Vault of the Forgotten Stars
Season 1

J.D. Coker

PUBLISHING

Contents

Gift of the Ancients

Gordon stood on the balcony of his villa, watching the evening sky. Another vessel burned through the atmosphere—the Omatrin Consortium's Deep Space Initiative, ferrying thousands offworld. They'd beaten him to FTL travel at scale, but their ships needed nav-beacons and established routes. The Void Sphere didn't.

He rubbed the back of his head where the surgical site had healed. The Chrominthium Core hummed beneath his skull—a sensation he'd learned to live with, though he'd never quite gotten used to it. When he turned his molecular awareness on, the world sharpened. The iron railing beneath his hands resolved into lattices of molecules, each one vibrating with kinetic energy he could redirect if he chose. The concrete beneath his feet became a crystalline matrix of calcium compounds and aggregate, individual atoms visible if he pushed his perception deep enough.

The headache came immediately. A dull pressure behind his eyes that would compress to a point if he maintained awareness too long. He'd learned his limits the hard way—the first activation had cost him two hours, his consciousness fragmenting across dimensions while Therasda found him seizing on the laboratory floor. The Core hadn't malfunctioned. Gordon's mind had simply tried to process too much, too fast. Molecular awareness was power, but the human psyche wasn't designed for it.

He'd trained since then. Trained Therasda and Nalen too. All three of them could maintain awareness for controlled periods without losing themselves. The key was discipline—knowing when to pull back before the drift set in, before your sense of self started to fragment.

The vision during the last Core adjustment had been different.

Nalen had been tweaking the frequency, routine calibration, when Gordon's awareness had expanded further than ever before. For a moment, his consciousness had stretched across impossible distances—touching hyperspace itself, perception bleeding into dimensions beyond the normal four. That's when something found him.

Not a transmission. An opportunistic intrusion. Whatever had been waiting out there—across the galaxy, tethered to a fortress in the Threxal system—felt Gordon's extended awareness brush against hyperspace and seized the connection.

Three hours gone. When Nalen finally pulled him out, Gordon had been reciting coordinates in a language he didn't know, blood streaming from his nose, his hands locked rigid on the armrests.

The Core didn't receive transmissions. It wasn't designed to. But during deep adjustments, when consciousness extended into hyperspace, it became vulnerable. A doorway that opened both ways. Whatever had pushed those coordinates into his head had waited for that exact moment—when Gordon's mind was spread thin across dimensions, defenses down, awareness reaching out into the dark. The probe data confirmed the coordinates were real—an anomaly in the Threxal system, exactly where the vision had shown him.

Someone wanted him to find that fortress. The question was why.

Therasda had trusted him enough to get the Core implanted even after watching Gordon's first catastrophic activation. Tonight, Gordon was asking him to trust again—to jump farther than they'd ever attempted, to coordinates that had been forced into his mind by something he didn't understand.

He crossed to a control panel and punched in a request for his jetcopter. The chrominthium strands woven through his prototype suit shimmered in his awareness—interdimensional resonance threading through the black material with its dark blue marbling. He grabbed a grav-disk from beside the panel, feeling the chrominthium veins pulse through the obsidian surface like phosphorescent roots.

Haeolt Corporation had filed three more chrominthium patents this week. Surface applications, nothing groundbreaking, but it meant Gordon's window was closing. If this anomaly was what he thought it was—a structure that bent physics itself—it could unlock applications Haeolt hadn't even dreamed of yet.

His jetcopter settled into a hover above the balcony—rotors tilted vertical for VTOL, the sleek cockpit barely large enough for two. Standard corporate transport, nothing special. Above, rotors beat against the evening air. Gordon snapped the disk upward and at its apex suspended it with his awareness, breaking off pieces while enlarging them into steps. He jumped, caught the first platform, and moved up the makeshift staircase to the cockpit.

Once seated, he reached out and pulled the grav-disk pieces back together, snapping the reassembled disk onto his right leg. The jetcopter banked toward the landing pad where Therasda and Nalen waited with the Void Sphere.

His hand tightened on the control stick. Whatever had forced those coordinates into his mind knew he'd come. Knew he'd be curious enough, ambitious enough, to follow the breadcrumb trail. That should worry him more than it did.

Hopefully, it would be another discovery to better humanity. Not another Thomas Haeolt exploitation scheme—profit over progress.

The main door to the Void Sphere was open and Gordon landed the jetcopter to the east on a nearby landing pad. He couldn't see Therasda or Nalen but he was sure that they were collecting gear and suiting up for their next mission.

The Void Sphere was similar in size to a space shuttle except shaped like its name implied. It didn't shine like chrome—instead there was a shimmer, almost like a force field. The chrominthium hull absorbed light and bent gravity around it, creating the distortion. Touch the surface without the right gloves and it would repel your hand.

After landing, he exited the cockpit and crossed toward the Void Sphere. Therasda's hover approached from the east—white, stock standard. Therasda didn't believe in owning anything he wasn't willing to lose and lived accordingly.

Nalen was quite different. He enjoyed the finer things in life as much as one could with the current affairs on Earth. His collection of literature was not as extensive as Gordon's but impressive. When not at work, he was clean cut and wore fine suits. His love of whiskey and cigars was far greater than even Therasda's.

As he disembarked from the hover, he wore the same prototype suit as Gordon and Therasda. For a man his size, standing tall at 6 feet 4 inches, Gordon was always impressed by how fluently he moved and by how he still found ways to work in cramped spaces, no matter what engineering task he was given. He was also an accomplished pilot and was a natural at using molecular awareness.

Gordon approached the ramp. "Andromeda," he said. "Threxal system."

Therasda straightened from the hull panel he'd been checking. "You're serious."

"The probe data..."

"The probe data's irrelevant if we can't get back." Therasda's voice was flat. "No beacons out there. No support. If the Sphere fails in Andromeda, Earth might as well be in another universe."

"The coordinates are solid," Nalen said. He was checking his datapad, not looking up. "If Gordon says they're accurate, they're accurate."

"You trust coordinates from a vision?" Therasda asked.

"I trust the math," Nalen said. "The hyperspace vectors align. It's feasible."

Therasda looked at Gordon for a long moment. "I watched you seize on that lab floor for two hours. Watched your eyes roll back, blood coming out your nose, while we couldn't do anything but wait. You're asking me to trust that whatever forced those coordinates into your head isn't doing the same thing right now, steering us into a trap."

Gordon met his eyes. "I am."

"Then we're idiots." Therasda shook his head, but there was something almost fond in the gesture. "You owe me an old-fashioned when we get back. The expensive stuff."

"Deal," Gordon said.

He entered the Void Sphere, and both Therasda and Nalen followed him. There were two rows of three seats, and Gordon sat in the far-left seat in the front row. When he did, the navigator podium rose from the ground. Attached to the top of it was the navigator helm.

Taking a deep breath and letting out a sigh, Gordon placed the navigator helm on his head as he lay back in the seat. Therasda sat in the front row with Gordon, while Nalen sat in the middle behind them. The ramp to the Void Sphere retracted and the door slid into place with a metallic click. The sound echoed through the Void Sphere. Silence followed as the pressure equalized.

As the navigator helm powered up, a blast shield lowered over Gordon's eyes and his molecular awareness turned on. In his mind's eye he could see the outside of the Void Sphere and how it was connected to the other dimensions outside of the original four. It was as if he was part of the Void Sphere and the dimensions were at his command.

He reached out with his awareness trying to visualize the location of the anomaly, the rocky small satellite suspended unnaturally in time and space. As the location's view came into focus, he created a tunnel through hyperspace.

The data forced itself in.

Computations flooded across his mind's eye—hyperspace jump vectors, gravitational eddies, dimensional resonance frequencies. Not from the helm. From outside.

Gordon understood immediately. His awareness was extended, interfacing with hyperspace through the navigator helm. He'd opened himself to the dimensional layers again. And just like during the Core adjustment, something was using that connection.

The same invasive touch that had planted coordinates in his skull during the adjustment, now guiding his navigation. Whatever wanted him at that fortress wasn't content to wait, it was steering him there, using Gordon's own extended awareness as the bridge.

The Void Sphere rose up from the launch pad, and he created a quantum tunnel from the surface of the planet that would provide enough speed to reach escape velocity. The Void Sphere would be in hyperspace, but planets' and stars' gravitational pull did seep into this realm, especially when on the surface of a planet.

This was the crucial part of the journey; if he didn't reach that point and acceleration, there were multiple catastrophic possibilities. The best worst-case scenario would be that the Void Sphere would enter Earth's orbit and need to be recovered by a spaceship.

As the Sphere hurtled through the quantum tunnel, Gordon focused through the building migraine. The beginning of these trips were always the worst—reality unraveling at the edges, his sense of self fragmenting across dimensions that shouldn't exist. One moment there was deep aching pain within his cells; the next, euphoric dissolution as his awareness expanded into hyperspace. He held on, teeth gritted, fighting the drift. The Core could show him infinity, but his mind would shatter long before he saw all of it.

When he had moments of clarity when not dealing with those sensations, he could see the path they were moving along through hyperspace towards their destination. He had successfully made it past Earth's influence on hyperspace and he was starting to become adept at using the Void Sphere.

The trip would only take a few hours but to Gordon and his companions, it would seem like days. He wasn't sure what they were experiencing and Nalen hadn't shared much about their earlier travels. He was oblivious to what was happening inside the Void Sphere because he had to stay focused so he could protect the Sphere from any outside forces.

The Void Sphere was close to reaching the system of Threxal. He could already feel how gravity from the main star in the system was reaching towards the quantum tunnel he had created. It was like great tendrils from a monstrosity that had been waiting for them in the cosmos since the beginning of time whose sole purpose was to consume passing entities.

They'd crossed into the system. Whatever had waited for them—tethered to that fortress, merged with hyperspace itself—no longer needed Gordon's awareness as a conduit. They were in range now. Direct manipulation.

Gordon pushed back with his mind and reinforced parts of the tunnel. No matter how he tried to reinforce it, a force kept pushing back, finding new ways to bypass his work, trying to insert its influence on the path the Void Sphere was taking. This wasn't gravity. This was intention. The same presence that had planted coordinates in his skull, now fully active within its domain.

Don't fight it...Gordon...

The voice drove into his mind like a spike. Gordon's awareness wavered, his grip on the tunnel loosening. Blood trickled from his nose inside the helmet.

I only want to converse with you about the intricacies of the path you have selected for your species...

Gordon tried to resist, to hold their course, but the presence was overwhelming—not stronger than him, but more skilled, more ancient. It knew hyperspace in ways Gordon had only begun to grasp. His headache flared white-hot. He was losing control.

A new path through hyperspace formed around them, coordinates shifting. Gordon could see the Void Sphere approaching the anomaly—still the same fortress from his vision, but its location had changed.

Through the navigator helm's connection, Gordon caught a flicker of something else: the presence straining, spreading itself thin. Reaching across that much space, holding the reroute stable while manipulating Gordon's tunnel—it was costing it something. Gordon could sense the effort, like feeling someone's grip weaken even as they maintained their hold. Whatever sapient being had spoken to him had rearranged space itself to intercept them. And it had hurt him to do it.

Instead of using his molecular awareness to maneuver the Void Sphere, he used it to recreate the images of outside the Sphere in his mind. In the far distance he could see the fortress from his vision. No light shone past it like other stars did when looking through a space telescope. The fortress had two main towers at the front corners of the walls. The architecture was Gothic, with tall arched entrances and intricate detailing on the top of the walls.

The rocky surface that it clung to was like a meteorite that came from a decrepit moon, stolen from a long-forgotten planet. It was unnatural and Gordon was filled with dread.

As they approached their destination the feeling intensified and Gordon eased out of his awareness. The migraine hit immediately, worse than usual. He'd been fighting that presence for hours, his mind stretched thin. Both Therasda and Nalen were at the ready, tension written across their faces; they felt it too.

The Void Sphere came to a stop and lowered to the ground. Normally the sound of touchdown would echo through the Sphere but there was silence. Without any commands from them, the door opened and there was no change in pressure.

Gordon pulled off the navigator helm with shaking hands. His vision wavered. He'd need a minute before he could stand without falling over.

The atmosphere should be acceptable. I await you and your team...

Therasda began to fasten his helmet to his suit but Gordon put up his hand.

"There will be no need for that Therasda," Gordon said. "I have been assured that we are only here for a brief conversation."

"Brief conversation?" Therasda said. "Who in the hell will we be talking to?"

"I'm not entirely sure but I have a feeling whatever it is or they are, is linked to our discovery of chrominthium." Gordon crossed the Void Sphere and placed his hands to the side of the frame of the door, leaning out. The fortress loomed over head as he surveyed the landscape outside of the Void Sphere. The terrain was oddly flat, a light brown horizon, with only the occasional ripple in the ground to break up the monotony. Throughout the landscape he could see the shimmer of chrominthium.

Gordon turned on his awareness. Below the ground level there was nothing but the interdimensional alloy to be found. He had never seen that amount of chrominthium, even on the planet of Chromwell where the first veins were discovered. Looking ahead, he saw that the interior structure of the fortress was similar. When he peered further within, there was a presence that was blocking him from viewing into the interior of where a courtyard would usually be located.

"Why aren't there any shadows?" Nalen asked. Both him and Therasda were standing on either side of Gordon. Their gaze was also in the direction of the structure and Gordon could sense that they were using their molecular awareness to observe the area around them.

"Well, it has to be because of the amount of chrominthium that is located here," Gordon said. He began moving toward the fortress. It appeared to only be around one hundred meters from their location but with how there seemed to be slightly different laws of physics here, he wasn't sure if that was an accurate approximation.

Therasda paused and pointed toward the top of the wall on the left side of the tower closest to them. On top of the wall there was a dark apparition. The presence had shifted from within the fortress to the wall.

He couldn't make out what the apparition was and it seemed to flicker—one moment radiating a soft yellow glow, the next pulling the light back in, struggling to maintain cohesion. Like watching someone catch their breath after exertion. The light was dimmer than the glow that illuminated the meteorite.

Gordon realized: the reroute had drained him. The presence had spent considerable energy intercepting them.

So you and your fellow travelers notice my presence now...This is a first...When I appeared to your kind millennia ago, they never noticed me or any of my kin.

What is it that you seek from us? Gordon replied back telepathically to the apparition. This was the first time that he had been able to reply back to the voice inside his mind.

Seek...It is what you have been seeking ever since you found our material on one of your planets. I will enlighten you when you reach my domicile. I cannot leave this place—my essence is bound to the fortress itself.

The presence hesitated, and Gordon felt the weight of that admission.

The fortress is more than stone. It's anchored across dimensional layers—a nexus where hyperspace intersects with your reality. I built it that way, in the days when I still had form and freedom. Now I'm merged with its structure. My consciousness extends through every chrominthium vein, every dimensional fold. What reaches out to you through hyperspace, what altered your course—that was me extending through the fortress's reach. But the substance of me, the coherent core of what I am, remains anchored here. Trapped in my own architecture.

The mental voice faltered. Exhaustion came through the link.

My reach extends only so far. Within this system, I can touch hyperspace, manipulate trajectories, project my awareness. But I cannot reach beyond Threxal's boundaries. I cannot affect precise events at distance. I cannot simply take what I need from my universe—I can barely perceive it from here, let alone manipulate matter across that boundary.

Gordon's mind worked through the implications. "The coordinates. You said you implanted them in my head. But if you can't reach beyond this system..."

I didn't reach out to you. Its mental voice carried something like satisfaction. *You reached out into hyperspace. During your Core adjustment, your consciousness extended beyond your body, beyond your planet, touching the dimensional boundaries I exist within. I simply... noticed. And when I found that open connection—your awareness spread thin across space, vulnerable, seeking—I used it as a bridge. You made yourself visible to me. Accessible.*

The vision hadn't been an attack from across the galaxy. It had been an opportunistic intrusion during a moment of weakness and Gordon had opened the door himself.

And each manipulation costs me. Hours, sometimes days to recover coherence.

"I can hear it now as well," Nalen said. Therasda was also nodding his head in agreement with what Nalen had said. "What creature is inside that fortress?"

Well, to be a creature one has to be created...I am Nyraxius, a whisper from the dark between stars.

"Great. It likes to speak in riddles," Therasda said with a look of disdain on his face. "Let's get this over with."

All three of them, almost in unison, moved towards the fortress. Halfway there, Therasda came to an abrupt stop. "It seems that in order to move we have to have our awareness turned on." His eyes phased back into a black and silver fluctuating pattern, as was the case with that anyone used the ability after Gordon had perfected it and trained the others.

When they arrived at the front of the fortress, the arched entrance loomed overhead. The same feeling of dread came over them as they moved to the tall doors that would lead them to the inner sanctum of the apparition.

On the front of the doors the words **Θησαυροφυλάκιο τῶν Ἐπιλελησμένων Ἄστρων** were written in a silver color, a stark contrast to the obsidian of the fortress walls and the sandy brown landscape surrounding them. It was as if molten chrominthium had been inlaid on the door eons ago.

"Thisavrofylakio ton epilelismenon astron," Gordon said, "which means Treasury of the Forgotten Stars or possibly Vault of the Forgotten Stars, depending on how poetic the author is. Doesn't seem to have any connection to any Ancient Greek lore that I'm aware of." He traced the writing with his right forefinger and then pushed the doors open. Surprisingly, they opened with ease and swung inwards farther than he had expected.

What lay before them was quite the scene. It was as if they were staring at the negative photo of a garden from a royal courtyard of ancient times. There were fountains sculpted in exquisite shapes. Some were in the form of large flowers and others were forest creatures, as if the birds and squirrels had come to water the courtyard.

The doors behind them shut forcefully and a loud crackling sound changed the colors of their surroundings back to their natural tones. Water began flowing from the fountains, and magnificent stone benches rose from the ground with a single throne like chair in the center.

The dark apparition flew in from off the wall where it had been and rested on the throne. The apparition changed from the shroud into a chiseled form of a man as if he was carved from the same marble that the fountains and the benches had been. He wore a set of purple robes and a matching cloak billowed over and behind the throne. Gordon had no idea what made the cloak move like that, there had been no evidence of any kind of wind or strong airflow since they had arrived on the anomaly.

"Take a seat if you wish, my honored guests," Nyraxius said in a playful tone. "There are certain details of your newfound abilities we should discuss."

Gordon crossed the courtyard and sat on the bench directly across from Nyraxius. Therasda was more cautious and stood to the right of Gordon. Nalen took a similar position and they both had detached their grav-disks and changed their suits into a more formidable armor like structure than the wet suit like composition.

"No need for hostilities," Nyraxius said, "Besides, who do you think gave you your precious chrominthium. That's a boring name for something so precious to you." He raised a hand and the grin on his face changed to a stern look as his lips straightened. Both of the grav-discs disappeared and reappeared to the side of his throne.

When he lowered his hand, the benches to the right and left of Gordon sprouted arms that reached out and grabbed both Therasda and Nalen. The arms pulled them backwards and made them sit. They retracted and melded back, returning the benches to their original shape.

"Why can't I move," Therasda said. "What a way to treat your honored guests."

"You can't move my dear Therasda because I have removed these pesky little creations of Gordon's from you." Nyraxius held all three of their Chrominthium Cores in the palm of his left hand. He held his hand chest level and the Cores levitated upward. A podium rose to Nyraxius's left. It also looked like it had been meticulously sculpted from marble. Intricate flower petals were all over its base and an angel like figure held the lectern at the top.

The Cores floated over to the podium. They didn't rest on the podium, they floated above it and rotated in a shifting figure eight pattern. "It will be much easier for us to discuss important matters if I have your full attention."

"Then lets discuss," Gordon said. He did his best not to show his frustration with Nyraxius. Before he had been curious about this being but now he was getting irritated with its contempt of them. He wasn't as brash as Therasda but he had no time for games or frivolous shows. "It's apparent that you have our attention. Why are we here?"

"To retrieve something from my universe," Nyraxius said. He rose from his chair and removed his cloak, placing it in the seat of the throne. As he paced, miniscule pieces fell off from his skin, only to fly upwards and rejoin him where strands of chrominthium shone from underneath. "A cylindrical device made of light blue crystal. It contains the consciousness of Araldenia—one of the Mélanes Tou Kósmou who discovered what you call chrominthium."

"The Dark Ones of the Cosmos," Gordon said. "Your people."

"How fitting that you know the ancient tongue," Nyraxius said. He stopped pacing. "We brought chrominthium to your universe by accident. When Araldenia returned with her discovery, I consumed her to gain that knowledge."

He held up his hand, chrominthium veins glowing beneath his marble skin.

"You think of it as a material. An alloy. But chrominthium is information made tangible—a substrate that encodes consciousness patterns and transmits them across dimensional boundaries. It doesn't just bend space or channel energy. It records thought, preserves identity, allows awareness to extend beyond the constraints of a single body or universe."

His marble form flickered, became pure chrominthium for an instant.

"Your Cores don't enhance your minds. They interface with chrominthium's informational substrate, letting you read and write reality at the molecular level. But chrominthium itself is the medium. Without it, consciousness stays trapped in meat. With it..." He gestured to himself. "We transcended. Built weapons of distributed awareness. Destroyed most of our universe in the wars that followed."

"And now you're exiled here," Nalen said.

"Trapped here," Nyraxius corrected. "I violated principles that cannot be forgiven." His form flickered, chrominthium veins pulsing beneath marble skin. "But that's not why I need you. Araldenia, before I consumed her, placed barriers throughout her universe. Traps keyed to my essence. If I cross that threshold, those barriers will capture what remains of me, fragment my consciousness across dimensions until nothing coherent exists." His hands clenched. "She knew I would come for her work eventually. She prepared accordingly."

"So send someone else," Gordon said, trying to reach his Core. The connection was gone.

"Who? You're the first beings to master chrominthium since we scattered it across your cosmos." Nyraxius's voice dropped. "You've touched it. Learned to channel it. You can cross where I cannot."

The shroud behind Nyraxius doubled in size. "For insurance that you retrieve what I ask for, I will hold Nalen hostage." From the ground a cage of chrominthium melded around Nalen.

Therasda rushed to the cage, running his hands frantically around the edges. "Gordon, don't..." The cage bubbled and enveloped him mid-sentence. His eyes met Gordon's through the chrominthium lattice. "Don't do it. Whatever he wants isn't worth..."

"Might as well contain him too," Nyraxius said. "Quite an annoying fellow, that one."

Therasda slammed his fist against the cage. No sound. The chrominthium absorbed the impact perfectly. He kept hitting it anyway, his face twisted with fury and something else—fear. Not for himself. For Gordon.

Gordon slowly inched his way towards the podium where their Chrominthium Cores were located.

"If you find the stasis chamber after you enter the interdimensional gateway, there should be a small cylindrical device made out of light blue crystal suspended inside it. There shouldn't be anyone guarding it because their resources are thin and they have blocked my access."

"So if you can't enter that gateway, then how do you think we will be successful?" Gordon replied. He wasn't far away, if only he could distract Nyraxius for a little bit longer.

"Because I can perceive but not manipulate at that distance." Nyraxius's voice carried frustration. "I can reach through hyperspace to affect ships, redirect trajectories. Crude, large-scale manipulations. But precision work? Retrieving a specific object from a specific chamber in another universe? That requires fine control I no longer possess. My reach extends far but my grip is weak. I need hands. Your hands."

"You won't be able to engage with your Core again after you enter and do as I ask." Nyraxius held up the three Cores, light catching on their surfaces. "If you don't, I will kill both of them and imprison you here to keep me company until some other poor soul finds me the same way that you did."

Gordon wanted nothing more than to shove that insufferable being back through the gateway. The grin Nyraxius was displaying was diabolical. Araldenia's barriers explained why he needed a proxy, but not why he wanted her device so desperately. What was in that crystal that was worth this much effort?

"Time to go, and do your best to retrieve my device."

With all of his might, Gordon tried to resist moving toward the gateway that had opened in the expanded shroud, but he slid toward it as Nyraxius raised the ground under his feet, constructing a slope with his version of molecular awareness that had to be greater in power than theirs had been.

As he neared it and was only inches away, the gateway was pulling him in. Instead of moving sideways, he felt like he was falling through a hole in the ground and darkness was enveloping him. The darkness wasn't even like that found deep within the bowels of a subterranean cavern, it was a different state of being, total isolation. The sheer terror caused Gordon to black out—he was no longer in his universe of origin, he was now somewhere between two universes.

✦ · · · ✦

Drifting in and out of consciousness, his original sensation of terror changed into awe. He had first felt total isolation, as if the Creator of the multiverse had picked him up and placed him in the darkest prison reserved for the most vile of creatures. After awhile though, his vision had adjusted, or what he thought was his vision, and he was able to see his surroundings as he assumed he was traveling to Nyraxius's universe.

He thought when he had discovered molecular awareness that he had reached the pinnacle of all experiences. He was wrong. This seemed to be like an out of body experience. One moment he was whole in form, could sense all of his body. The next, he felt his cells separate and he was detached from his physique and could inspect every single cell of his body. He wasn't sure what he was surrounded by either, it was heavier than air but lighter than water. There was a haze like quality to it and there were tiny particles of light that floated by every so often.

To Gordon it also felt like he wasn't going in one particular path or direction. Whenever his cells were separated, occasionally one of the light particles touched one of them. There was mild pain at first but then euphoria. It was as if this realm had the beginning particles of star dust and was responsible for the stars created in the connecting universes. He wasn't sure if he ever wanted to leave this realm.

Time was of no consequence here either. He couldn't tell how much time had passed, to him it felt possible that it could have been an eternity. In the distance, Gordon could see a similar dark gateway as had been back in the fortress. The outline of the next universe came into focus beyond the gateway and he remembered his purpose.

Retrieve the small cylindrical device made out of light blue crystal suspended inside the stasis chamber.

Gordon could still hear the sound of Nyraxius's voice when he thought of that phrase that reminded him of his task ahead. He wasn't sure what to expect when he reached the other universe. Hopefully he would retrieve what Nyraxius wanted and find a way to stop him from whatever scheme he was planning.

As he had entered the gateway prior, Gordon felt as if he was falling into it again, with the same darkness and isolation...His consciousness soon faded.

+ · · · +

Gordon tried to stand but had no legs. His center of mass pulled sideways as he rose—if rising was the word for whatever his body was doing.

Twenty appendages writhed below him. His appendages. Gordon forced himself to look. Tentacles, each one terminating in suckers he could feel contracting. When he focused on one, his perspective shifted, vision multiplying. Twenty viewpoints available simultaneously.

His stomach lurched. He focused on the laboratory around him, on categorizing, on anything but what he'd become. He must have somehow changed into the original form of the Mélanes Tou Kósmou as they had been in this universe.

This had been different than their experience when they traveled to Gordon's universe. He was puzzled by this but it must have been because he had already had contact with chrominthium and had even learned how to channel its energy.

The room was like a laboratory and every thing was in the shades of a negative of a photo like when they had first stepped inside the courtyard in the fortress on the anomaly. The tables were taller than what was the standard for humans and he soon found out the reason why. When he tried moving, his round bulbous like segmented body floated through the air, or what he assumed was this universes version of air. Their were multiple valves along the under and upside of his carapace that opened and closed, regulating the exchange of gases that kept him afloat.

Gordon tried to remain calm but he felt as if he was going to be sick. He didn't even know if his current state would allow him to regurgitate anything but if he had been human, he would have thrown up whatever had been on his stomach. He focused and recited positive mantras in his mind that he reserved for moments like this. At least he had his mind operating at peak performance, and he felt as if he had acquired more knowledge each moment that he spent in this new realm of reality.

Although this universe was devoid of any color like back home, it was easier for Gordon to calculate exact distances of every item. His perception had expanded—thousands of gradations between black and white, each distinguishable and categorizable. He had to have a smaller brain in each appendage as well to allow him this perspective.

Had H.P. Lovecraft somehow tapped into this universe? The thought struck him with unsettling clarity. The man had denied using hallucinogens in his letters, but maybe he hadn't needed them. Maybe he'd glimpsed this realm in dreams or visions—tentacled beings, non-Euclidean geometry, consciousness distributed across impossible forms.

The more time he spent in the laboratory he knew where everything was. There were beakers made out of different materials than glass, and as he looked at them he could see their molecular structure simultaneously alongside his normal view. His molecular awareness had been upgraded, and he didn't see any chrominthium nearby or sense that it was located anywhere inside of him.

When he noticed the exits from the laboratory, one of them caught his attention. In writing over the door it said, **Stasis Chamber, proceed with caution**. He floated toward the octagon shaped door that was midway up the wall and peered with his awareness into the next room. Inside, the room was rectangular in shape and there was a type of chamber in the center. He couldn't tell what was inside, there was shielding that was blocking his awareness as if whatever was inside was off limits to any passerby.

As he approached the door it opened and he floated through the door with half of his tentacles trailing behind him while the others went ahead to observe if there was anything he should be aware of before entering. There was no presence so far of any other being like Nyraxius and some of what he had been talking about must have been factual. If their universe was well populated, he would have been sure to see whoever owned or guarded this facility by now. There also appeared to be a power supply nearby that Gordon had never encountered before.

The stasis chamber extended deep into the wall. If the item that Nyraxius wanted was far back, Gordon wasn't sure if he'd be able to see it through whatever shielding blocked his awareness.

Gordon reached out with four of his tentacles to search the front panel of the chamber. There wasn't any more writing that depicted anything particular like there had been over the door in the first room he had arrived in. There were parallel lines that had been cut into the panel and every so often there were oval grooves where the suckers on the end of his front tentacles could fit. When the suckers fit inside, he noticed a certain pattern and instinctively he pressed them in a way that felt natural.

When he pushed back from the grooves, a loud sound of pressure released, echoing throughout the room. This had been the first sound that he had noticed since arriving here. He hadn't realized this at first as he was still getting accustomed to this universe and the similarities and the differences between the two. A line appeared in the center of the chamber from top to bottom. At first it was grey in color and then it changed to light blue.

The light blue line changed into a light source that illuminated the room with color. Everything in the room began to take on color patterns that were more familiar to him. The chamber went from a light shade of grey to a silver tone. His skin changed from a darker shade of grey to a swirl of iridescent blue and purple hues. Alongside the wall further towards the back of the right side of the chamber, there were brown and green plants that floated in the air and a robot with a suspensor motor hovered as it watered them.

The door to the chamber creaked loudly as it retracted inwards and inside suspended in the middle was the cylindrical light blue crystal. Another light turned on, this one an orange hue and behind the crystal was another being like him. Gordon started to retreat and posed his tentacles in a defensive position.

"Curious," the Mélanes Tou Kósmou said. The voice wasn't as deep as Nyraxius—Gordon thought it could pass as feminine. Several small eyes opened on the front of her carapace, studying him. "You wear our form. Others came in their own skin."

"Others?" Gordon asked. "Nyraxius said..."

"Nyraxius says many things. Some true, some useful, rarely both." Her tentacles undulated in patterns that might have been language. "You're wondering if I'm Araldenia. If I'm what he claims I am. The answer is...partially."

Gordon tried to parse that. "He said he consumed you."

"He consumed one version." She floated closer, circling him slowly. The small eyes blinked in sequence—left to right, then right to left. "Consciousness copies easily in chrominthium. I shed carapaces the way you shed skin cells. What he ate was... outdated."

"Then the device..."

"Contains what he thinks he wants." She stopped circling. "You're here because your friends are hostages. You think you have one choice. Take the device, return, save them. Yes?"

"Yes."

"Nyraxius believes sending you here was strategic. A test. But he doesn't understand what you've become by crossing." She drifted toward the chamber, tentacles reaching for the crystal. "In your universe, you channel kinetic energy through will. Here, you've learned to do it without chrominthium at all. Do you know why?"

Gordon looked down at his tentacled form. "No."

"Because consciousness itself is the substrate. Chrominthium is an interface—it encodes, transmits, preserves awareness across dimensional boundaries. But once you understand the principles..." She tilted her carapace. "You can manipulate reality directly. The Core, the chrominthium, they're training wheels. Frameworks to help biological minds grasp what distributed consciousness can do."

She held the crystal between several tentacles.

"This device contains knowledge. Mathematical proofs of those principles. Designs for consciousness architecture. Also...me. Or versions of me. Fragments encoded in crystal lattice. Enough that Nyraxius will believe he has what he seeks."

"What does he seek?"

"Validation. Power. Revenge. The usual degradations." Her eyes closed in sequence. "What do you seek, Gordon Feuridi?"

"To save my friends."

"And after?"

Gordon hesitated. "To understand what we've found. What chrominthium really is."

"Then take this." She extended the crystal toward him. "But know: Nyraxius is trapped in your universe for reasons. Bringing this to him gives him tools. Whether he can use them..." Her carapace shifted as she angled her head. "That depends on variables I'm still calculating."

"You're not going to stop me."

"Stop you?" Something that might have been amusement rippled through her carapace. "You woke me at precisely the correct time. I've been waiting for a Shaper to cross. The astronochron showed me this moment long ago.Or it will show me. Causality is... negotiable here."

"I don't understand."

"You will." She floated toward the far door. "After you deal with Nyraxius. After you find what's waiting in Barnard's Galaxy."

"What's in Barnard's Galaxy?"

"The reason its structure is irregular." Her tentacles reached for the door. "The reason chrominthium exists at all. The reason your species evolved pattern-recognition consciousness instead of distributed processing." She looked back at him with all her eyes at once. "Take the device. Learn what you can. But Gordon... don't trust what you learn too quickly. Truth takes longer than data."

The door opened and she was gone.

Gordon stood alone with the crystal, unsure if Araldenia had helped him or used him, or if those were even different things to a being that experienced time non-linearly.

He reached out with his awareness. Changing back without chrominthium—without the Core's stabilization—would be like performing surgery on himself while conscious. He had to remember every detail of his human form: the exact arrangement of organs, the neural pathways, the proportion of his limbs. One mistake and he'd reassemble incorrectly.

He channeled kinetic energy from nearby molecules and began. The transformation felt like being torn apart and reassembled simultaneously. Twenty tentacles condensing into two arms, two legs. His distributed consciousness compressing back into a single brain. The pain was exquisite—every nerve ending firing as it reformed.

Gordon screamed. His vocal cords were still forming but the sound came out anyway, distorted and alien. He held the image of his human body in his mind, forced matter to comply. Bones crystallized. Muscles wove together. Skin sealed over raw tissue.

He collapsed onto the floor, gasping, fully human again. Naked. Trembling. But human.

He rearranged molecules from the generator of the stasis chamber—chrominthium, thank god, something familiar—and grabbed fibers from the plants to wrap himself with a new suit like the prototype he'd originally worn to the anomaly. The color was different though. Instead of the dark blue marbling it was in the swirl pattern of iridescent blue and purple matching the color of the Mélanes Tou Kósmou skin.

A reminder. He'd been something else. He could be something else again.

Thankful that he was now back to his original self, or as close to it as he had tried to make, Gordon crossed the room and stood before the cylindrical light blue crystal.

As he drew closer to the crystal, he could swear Araldenia's presence was still here and then when he actually tried to retrieve it...Mathematical equations burned across his vision. Molecular structures assembled faster than thought. The sensation of Araldenia's consciousness coalesced with his. He staggered but didn't fall.

I will be your guide from time to time, Araldenia said to him in his mind. *Put an end to Nyraxius and his biddings and then come find me in Barnard's Galaxy in the Thon-Variis system. There is a specific reason why that galaxy has an irregular structure.*

As a renowned physicist he knew about Barnard's Galaxy and its structure but this statement intrigued him. He would travel there next after he made sure that his friends and his organization back on Earth was still intact. It wouldn't surprise him if his chief competitor Thomas Haeolt used his absence to try and come up with another scheme to derail his current projects.

This time he walked willingly towards the gateway that would lead back to his universe and entered. He had a better idea of how to steer his course once he entered but hoped that time back in his universe was relevant to the amount he had spent here.

+ · · · +

With the sky above the fortress opening up amidst a shower of crackling energy, Gordon entered his home universe and landed with a loud crash atop the fortress walls. He had slowed down his descent and displaced the inertia at the right time, causing all but one pillar of the wall to tumble down, the one he was standing on. If this entrance hadn't alarmed Nyraxius to his presence, Therasda and Nalen must have already subdued him.

While in transit between universes, he had studied more of the data that Araldenia had shared with him and some of her consciousness had spilled inside his. She hadn't transferred it there as far as he could tell, but he could feel her presence and found that reassuring. He would need all the assistance he could to take on Nyraxius. He was still master of the anomaly and there had to be properties here that Gordon hadn't taken into consideration.

He leaped off of the top of the wall down into the courtyard, grabbing the debris from the wall with his awareness. He had the debris continuously spin around him acting as a shield to protect him from any unseen projectiles that Nyraxius might send his way.

"Ah you have returned, " Nyraxius said as he stepped around part of the crumbled wall that had fell into the courtyard. "Neat tricks you picked up on your journey. I'm guessing you have my item but plan on keeping it for yourself."

"You are correct," Gordon said. He sent the debris that had been rotating around him in a trajectory aimed towards Nyraxius. He pulled other molecules from around the debris and changed it into projectiles with explosive hollow point tips.

Nyraxius had a look on his face that he was impressed with what Gordon had done. If he was impressed though, he wasn't worried. When the projectiles were almost at the point of impact, Nyraxius translated his matter right behind Gordon. The projectiles hit the benches and fountains that were in the courtyard spraying both of them with broken pieces of marble.

"You'll have to do better than that, Gordon if you want to catch me off guard." He hit Gordon with his fist, or what Gordon thought was his fist, but as he looked down a sharp blade had punctured his right arm. He pulled away from him and leapt as hard as he could. While he was in the air, he used his awareness to raise the ground behind and in front of him, trying to guess Nyraxius next movement.

As if he knew what Gordon was trying to do, Nyraxius reached out with his awareness and crumbled both mounds. He then translated himself into the 5th dimension, searched for Gordon with his awareness, and then blinked back in, right next where he was going to land.

"Oh shit," Gordon said. He changed the structure in his feet into slabs of plascrete, adjusting his legs to be able to absorb any impact. Nyraxius hadn't expected his move, and Gordon's right foot hit his head and the left on his shoulder.

"Well it's obvious, if I don't end this soon, you might stand a chance," Nyraxius said as he threw Gordon off of him with exceptional force.

Gordon blocked the follow-up strike—Nyraxius trying to crush his chest—pushing back with molecular awareness. But in that moment of divided focus, Nyraxius seized control of Gordon's torso. Gordon's chest cavity elongated against his will, forming a sail-like structure. Nyraxius pulled air molecules from around them, using the deformed chest as a sail to launch Gordon into the air.

While he was sailing through the air, Gordon regained control. He protected his vital organs, healed the puncture wound in his right arm, and condensed his chest cavity back to its original form. He displaced the inertia from his fall.

The migraine hit like a hammer. He'd pushed his awareness too far, too fast—healing, manipulating matter, all without the Core's stabilization. His vision swam, reality blurring at the edges. The drift was coming. He had minutes before his mind started fragmenting.

He used the kinetic energy buildup to phase shift as far away from Nyraxius as he could and also sent a false signal in another direction hoping Nyraxius wouldn't predict correctly.

He reappeared on the other side of the only support pillar, gasping, his hands trembling. Blood trickled from his nose. One more jump. Maybe two before the drift took him. He phase shifted again, sending his matter toward where Therasda and Nalen had been imprisoned. As he blinked back into the courtyard, Gordon sundered the chrominthium cage surrounding them and splintered the leftover pieces, creating another shield of thousands of razor sharp projectiles.

Nyraxius was standing on top of the pillar as he had been late in tracking Gordon's movement. His form fluctuated between the chiseled marble man and the apparition—unstable, like a broadcast signal losing coherence.

Gordon could see it now: Nyraxius was overextended. The hyperspace reroute had drained him—he'd said it would take days to recover that kind of reach, and he'd spent it all bringing them here. Now he was reduced to this: physical combat, matter manipulation within the fortress. No long-range tricks left. No warping them away. Just desperate, direct confrontation.

Maintaining his physical form while fighting was costing him more than he wanted to show. The hairline fractures in his marble skin were spreading, exposing chrominthium light beneath.

He was losing cohesion. Spreading himself too thin across too many dimensional layers. Gordon tried to remember anything he'd learned from Araldenia's device that could accelerate Nyraxius's collapse, force him back into pure apparition where he'd have less power to hurt them.

Gordon had taken too long to free his friends and think about his next move. As he turned to focus back on Nyraxius, the surrounding projectile shield was parted to either side, and two spear-like strands of chrominthium skewered him on each shoulder, knocking him over and then pinning him to the ground. Gordon tried to send the projectiles at Nyraxius, but they fell.

"Run back to the Void Sphere," Gordon shouted at Therasda and Nalen.

Neither of them moved. Therasda's eyes met his. That look said everything.

Gordon didn't have time to argue.

He began fashioning new upgraded Chrominthium Cores for each of them, drawing on knowledge from Araldenia's device. Pain lanced through his skull. Creating Cores—actual functional Cores—while pinned and bleeding, while his consciousness threatened to scatter across dimensions. But he couldn't let them die here.

He phase shifted the first Core inside Therasda's head, mapping neural pathways, interfacing with synapses. One micron off and Therasda's brain would hemorrhage. Gordon's vision tunneled. Blood poured from both nostrils now. Second Core. Nalen. The world tilted sideways but Gordon held his awareness together through sheer spite.

He had been successful in reinstating their Cores, and as Nyraxius stood over him, he watched as they moved away from the debris of the destroyed fortress walls. Gordon's hands wouldn't stop shaking. He could feel his mind fraying at the edges, reality becoming negotiable.

Nyraxius reached down and retrieved the cylindrical light blue crystal that was attached to Gordon's suit on his left leg. He held the crystal in the air with his right hand and with his left he moved it back and forth as if he was conducting a symphony. With each movement of his hand upwards one of the razor sharp chrominthium projectiles rose from the ground and with the downward movement, it hurtled towards Gordon.

Projectile after projectile was hitting Gordon and when each one struck a targeted nerve point, it was all he could do to not yell out in pain. Biting his bottom lip he tried his best to focus, to think of some way to fight back but it was as if he had spent all of his energy with his previous attempts at felling Nyraxius.

Standing over Gordon, Nyraxius ceased sending projectiles up and down Gordon's body. He knelt and wiped blood from Gordon's face. "I am going to enjoy finishing this." He pulled one of the chrominthium spears as hard as he could from Gordon. Taking his time to stare at Gordon and spin the spear in his hand, he then raised it with the tip pointing straight at Gordon's chest.

Gordon's mind was racing. He didn't want to die like this, especially when Therasda and Nalen might not be able to make it back to Earth without him. It had been his curiosity that had caught them unaware, and there was no telling what Nyraxius's plans were for them if he failed.

Send him to me, Araldenia said to Gordon telepathically. He was shocked at first when she spoke to him. She must be more powerful than Nyraxius to speak to someone between universes despite his claims. Gordon knew that it could also be from the link the two shared and the proximity of her device. Whatever was the case, he was glad that she was at least a temporary ally. He didn't know if she also had ulterior motives for wanting Nyraxius sent back to their universe.

With blood pouring out from multiple wounds, Gordon reached deep—deeper than he'd ever gone, past the limits of human consciousness, into the quantum substrate itself. Opening a gateway between universes without the Void Sphere, without preparation, while his mind was already fragmenting from overuse. This would either work or his consciousness would scatter across dimensions and never reassemble.

The gateway tore open behind Nyraxius. Gordon screamed. It felt like his skull was splitting apart, like every neuron was firing simultaneously and burning out. Reality fractured into overlapping images—he could see multiple timelines, multiple versions of this moment. His sense of self started dissolving.

Nyraxius's look of enjoyment turned to consternation as he must have felt what Gordon had done. He thrust the spear at Gordon's chest.

Pushing as hard as he could, Gordon shattered the spear with his awareness, surprising Nyraxius and he catapulted himself in his direction. His right shoulder, the one that had still been pinned down had a huge whole with the right arm barely attached.

His left shoulder contacted the center of Nyraxius's chest and he latched on to as much of the debris as he could that was surrounding them. Gordon sent it all in Nyraxius direction and Nyraxius stumbled backwards to the gateway, grabbing on to the sides of it with both hands, trying to prevent himself from entering.

Chunks of marble were sloughing off Nyraxius's arms where he gripped the gateway's edge. His form was unraveling—too much exertion, too much matter manipulation. He wasn't the overwhelming force he'd been at the start. He was desperate, barely holding coherence.

Gordon fell to his knees. He had lost a large amount of blood as he hadn't been able to try and fix his wounds while he was fixated on Nyraxius. He tried to stand and was unable to and he was feeling dizzy.

Nyraxius steadied himself, his form solidifying slightly through sheer will. Araldenia must have also been involved and was trying to pull him inwards, but without Gordon continuing his assault, Nyraxius started moving away from the gateway's edge.

"Hey asshole."

Therasda stepped out from behind the rubble, his face twisted with cold fury. Gordon had seen that expression exactly once before—on the lab floor, when Therasda thought he was watching his friend die. "That's my friend you're torturing." He had his grav-disk in his hand and threw it at Nyraxius.

The disk shattered mid-flight. Therasda split the pieces into three groupings, each one attacking from a different angle. Nyraxius dodged the first two, but the third hit him square in the throat, sending chunks of marble and chrominthium flying.

Nalen had quietly approached from a different direction and when Nyraxius raised both of his hands to grab his throat, Nalen grabbed the sides of his chest and pushed him into the gateway. The gateway began to close around Nyraxius and Nalen tried to pull both of his arms free. At the last second, Nyraxius reached out and grabbed Nalen's right arm. The gateway closed around Nalen's arm and it severed it in the middle of his forearm. He reached with his left hand and clasped it around the perfectly cauterized stump. He didn't cry out in pain and only stared at where the gateway had been, still in shock, the pain not registering yet.

While the two of them had attacked Nyraxius, Gordon had used his awareness to stop his bleeding, closing the wounds. He slowly reconstructed plasma, red blood cells, white blood cells, and platelets within his blood vessels. He could feel his strength returning and he was no longer in critical condition. He knew that he must look like hell but he didn't care about that at the moment. Nyraxius was no longer around them and hopefully he was in Araldenia's custody.

What benches and fountains hadn't been demolished from their fight, were now beginning to turn into molten liquid. All three of them stood up and congregated near each other. The ground began to shake and boulder sized patches started rising from the ground. The last pillar of the fortress wall fell.

"I don't think we have much time to make it back to the Void Sphere," Gordon said. He was looking back in the direction where it had landed. He could sense it with his awareness. "Without Nyraxius here to be at the seat of power, this realm of his making will not hold its properties." Beams of light broke through the initial haze that had permeated the anomaly. The temperature was dropping radically and Gordon shaped a flight helmet that looked as if it was growing from the neck of his suit to surround his head. The other two did the same and they all made sure that they no longer had any exposed skin.

"Do not move," Gordon said. He had taken a balanced posture as if he was readying himself for an unseen impact. "I am going to phase shift us to the Void Sphere. When we arrive, I'll need you both to use your awareness to reinforce the sides of the Sphere, while I try to pilot it as quick as possible."

In his mind he saw the location of the Void Sphere. He reached out with his awareness and took into account every detail of their matter composition. Three bodies. Trillions of cells each. Every molecule had to stay coherent, had to reassemble correctly.

His mind stretched across impossible distances. He could feel Therasda's neural patterns, Nalen's compromised circulatory system where the arm had been severed, his own damaged tissues. All of it mapped, all of it held in his awareness simultaneously while he blinked them into the fifth dimension.

The world went white.

Gordon's consciousness scattered across dimensions, experiencing the jump from three perspectives at once. He was Gordon and Therasda and Nalen, three sets of memories, three minds screaming as reality dissolved. He held on—held all of them together by sheer force of will—and reassembled them at the cellular level inside the Void Sphere.

Gordon opened his eyes, gasping, and immediately vomited blood. His hands shook uncontrollably. That had nearly shattered him. He'd felt his identity fragmenting, pieces of him scattering into hyperspace. Only luck—or Araldenia's gift—had let him pull himself back together.

But they were here. All three of them. Alive.

He staggered to the first seat behind the navigator podium, barely able to walk straight. The fact that he'd done it flawlessly—that all three of them had their organs in the right places, their neurons firing correctly—seemed impossible. He'd translated organic matter other than his own for the first time, and somehow hadn't killed them all.

The navigator helm had already been powered up beforehand by Nalen and Gordon placed it on his head as he sat down. Therasda was to the left side of the row of chairs, while Nalen was in front with his hands touching the sides of the Void Sphere. Both of them were concentrating, trying their best to assist Gordon.

The blast shield of the helm lowered and Gordon took one last look with his mind's eye on the outside of the Void Sphere. The meteorite like landscape that the fortress had been on was broken up into a multitude of comet like shapes. It was as if this part of the universe was reclaiming the space that had previously been its own, purging all of the effects the anomaly Nyraxius had created.

Right before Therasda and Nalen could no longer hold on with their molecular awareness, Gordon created a quantum tunnel using all of the data of Earth's location along with the proper hyperspace jump vector. He eased it into the tunnel and with his mind searched around the Void Sphere, looking for any other influences on hyperspace like what he experienced before they had arrived at Nyraxius's lair.

Unlike other times where he had to maintain focus while piloting the Void Sphere he was able to take off the navigator helm so he could check on his team. Therasda and Nalen had sit down in the row behind him, leaning back in exhaustion with their legs fully extended.

"I apologize for putting us through this," Gordon said while deconstructing his helmet, melding it back into the neck of the suit. "I think you both deserve a raise and a significant stake in my company."

"Damn right we do," Therasda said. He leaned back, closing his eyes. "When we land, I'm drinking your entire top shelf. You can deduct it from my raise."

Nalen laughed, but it came out shaky. He looked at his hand—the one that was still whole. "We almost didn't make it back."

The words hung in the air. No one contradicted him.

"I know," Gordon said quietly. He was still trembling, blood crusted under his nose. "I know."

Therasda opened his eyes. "That thing in your head, the vision, the coordinates. You said something wanted you there." His voice was careful. "Do you know what it was yet?"

"Desperation," Gordon said. "Nyraxius was desperate. Trapped. And we walked right into it because I had to know. Had to follow the lead." He met Therasda's eyes. "I'm sorry."

"Don't." Therasda's jaw was tight. "We chose to get on this ship. We chose to follow you through that fortress. We chose to stay when you told us to run." He looked at Nalen, then back to Gordon. "But next time...and there will be a next time with you.We plan better. We assume the worst. We don't give anyone leverage over us like that again."

"Agreed," Nalen said. His voice was steadier now.

"Agreed," Gordon said.

The Void Sphere hummed around them, carrying them home through hyperspace. None of them spoke for a long time. There was nothing left to say that wouldn't sound inadequate.

Finally, Gordon broke the silence. "I also need to tell you about where Nyraxius sent me. It will be hard for you to believe at first, but the knowledge I gained should give us an edge against our competitors."

+ · · · +

The journey back to Earth had been uneventful. Gordon was able to steer the Void Sphere without being connected to it with the navigator helm, and shockingly when they landed on the landing pad near his villa, they had only been gone for four days of Earth's time.

The door to the Void Sphere opened and Gordon motioned for them to exit before he did. He started scanning the Sphere to make sure that none of Nyraxius handiwork was attached to the craft. Satisfied that he didn't need to immediately quarantine anything, he followed Therasda and Nalen outside.

Night had fallen and there was a strong breeze that brought the smell of leaves. Fall was well underway and the nearby trees had already turned. Gordon was happy to have his feet on solid ground on their home planet.

They'd been gone four days and Nalen had lost his arm. Gordon had been pinned down, bleeding out, while his friends fought an interdimensional being to save him. The reconstructed hand looked perfect—every finger, every joint articulated flawlessly. But it wasn't the same. Couldn't be. Gordon had rebuilt it from memory and Araldenia's knowledge, but he hadn't been there when Nalen first learned to grip a wrench, hadn't felt the unique neural pathways that made Nalen's hands so skilled at delicate work.

Nalen kept flexing the fingers, over and over. Testing the response time, the tactile feedback.

"Does it feel right?" Gordon asked quietly.

"It feels like someone else's hand." Nalen's voice was flat. "The commands go out, the hand responds, but there's this... delay. Like I'm operating a glove instead of living in my own skin."

Therasda turned away sharply. Gordon knew what he was thinking—he'd been right there when it happened, watching the gateway close around Nalen's arm.

"I can adjust the neural mapping. Fine-tune the..."

"It's not about the mapping." Nalen finally stopped flexing and let the hand drop to his side. "It feels like someone else's hand. Like I'm operating a glove instead of living in my own skin." He looked at the reconstructed fingers. "My actual hand is still in that fortress. Or scattered across dimensions. Or whatever happens to matter when an interdimensional gateway closes on it." He met Gordon's eyes, but there was no anger there. Just resignation. "I know you did your best. But we can't reconstruct what we lost."

"Take a week," Gordon said. "Not a few days. A week minimum. More if you need it."

Therasda looked at him, then nodded. "A week."

Nalen was already testing the reconstructed hand again, forcing it through a series of complex finger patterns. "What's in Barnard's Galaxy?"

"Araldenia," Gordon said. "She said to find her in the Thon-Variis system. Said there's a reason that galaxy has an irregular structure."

"Another fortress?" Therasda asked.

"Maybe. I don't know yet."

"Then we plan better next time," Nalen said. He finally got his thumb joint right and lowered his hand. "More data. Better contingencies."

"Agreed," Gordon said.

Therasda didn't yet have a glass of whiskey in his hand but Nalen had brought out cigars from the nearby hover, and he hadn't hesitated in lighting one of them up.

"We will see you soon, boss," Therasda said. Nalen remained quiet as he continued testing his hand.

"Yes you will," Gordon said. He watched as they entered Therasda's hover. The hover took of in the direction of the main residential compound but then Therasda turned it around and pulled sideways to Gordon.

The passenger seat window lowered and Nalen leaned out, extending his good arm to Gordon. "I think you forgot something. I managed to grab it and attach it to my Shaper suit before you phase shifted us." In his hand was the cylindrical light blue crystal. It was still glowing, but instead of a steady glow, the light was pulsing. The effect was calming to Gordon and he gladly accepted it from Nalen. "See you soon."

They took off and Gordon made his way back to his jetcopter. The ride wasn't long back to his villa and he would put it in autopilot so he could continue to think about his next plan of actions for his corporation.

+ · · · +

Gordon was on the balcony of his villa enjoying a quiet evening. A day had passed and he was already counting down the days when Therasda and Nalen would return to his main lab. He had his Shaper suit on and he had kept the swirl pattern of iridescent blue and purple. The rest of his Shapers—Therasda, Nalen, and those he would soon be recruiting—would use the original black with blue marbling color for their suits. He needed a reminder of the form he had taken on his journey to the Mélanes Tou Kósmou universe and would use that in his primers for his new recruits.

Above, the evening sky was clear. No launches tonight. The Omatrin Consortium moved thousands along established routes. Gordon's path lay elsewhere—deeper into questions most people didn't know to ask yet.

He turned from the railing and moved inside his personal quarters. The room was pristine, unlike his laboratory, since he didn't spend much time here. On a shelf near the gravity bed centered on the rear wall of the room he had placed Araldenia's device. It was in a protective case and the only way it could be released was by a combination of a retinal and fingerprint scan.

The mathematical proofs inside would take months to parse. The consciousness fragments longer still. And somewhere in Barnard's Galaxy, Araldenia—or versions of her—waited with answers about why chrominthium existed at all.

Gordon turned on his awareness. The device resolved into crystalline lattices, information density beyond anything human technology could achieve. Araldenia had said truth takes longer than data. He'd start with the data anyway.

Six months ago he'd sat in a laboratory chair and lost himself staring at molecules. Now he'd crossed universes, worn an alien form, and returned with knowledge that could reshape what humanity understood about consciousness itself. The Core hummed beneath his skull—no longer frightening, just another tool.

He had work to do.

Traitor's Influence

Rolling grasslands stretched for miles around Gavon Elmin, broken only by scattered stands of trees. Wildflowers he couldn't identify filled the air with a cloying sweetness—off-world scents that marked him as an intruder here. Lealvi, a Vethalian homeworld, protected by interplanetary treaty. No human colonies. Exploitation forbidden.

And here he stood, lying to everyone he met.

Gavon bent the light molecules around himself, redirecting photons with his molecular awareness as a patrol passed within twenty meters. The Vethalians moved with characteristic grace, their scanning equipment held loosely as they talked among themselves. He held his breath despite the unnecessary caution—his awareness rendered him effectively invisible—and waited for them to crest the hill.

When they disappeared from view, he resumed his descent. Grass brushed against his knees, each blade a potential sensor in this world where plants and machines merged through vethalian bioengineering. He extended his awareness downward with each step, checking for scanning nodes buried in the soil. The Vethalians manipulated their hybrid devices through pheromones, which made Gavon's molecular awareness nearly useless for detecting them in their dormant state. He could see the molecular structure of chrominthium and carbon fiber easily enough, but not whether a device waited for the chemical trigger to activate.

The diplomatic mission provided convenient cover—five Shapers acting as security detail for a human ambassador negotiating mining rights. It was perfectly legitimate and utterly boring, the kind of mission that wouldn't draw scrutiny.

The kind of mission that let Gavon hunt a traitor.

Ilsidore Triln. The name wouldn't leave Gavon's mind. He'd trained the boy himself—watched him ace every assessment at the academy, master molecular awareness faster than any initiate in twenty years. Then one day Ilsidore vanished without a trace.

Three months later, a terrorist attack on Hevron VII. Dead scattered across a market square. And among the rubble, a calling card—molecular signatures only a Shaper could leave. Ilsidore wanted them to know. He was announcing his betrayal.

The Order of Infinity hadn't produced a rogue Shaper in two centuries. The last one ignited a star, destroyed an entire solar system. The resulting fines nearly bankrupted the Order. More than that, it shattered trust. Even now, species across the intergalactic community viewed Shapers with suspicion. One madman with molecular awareness could end civilizations.

Gavon couldn't let that happen again.

He reached the base of the hill and pressed his back against an Ilmio tree. The diplomatic quarters sat five kilometers north—too far to reach quickly if something went wrong. He'd altered his Shaper suit to match Lealvi's vegetation, green and brown camouflage with his awareness providing additional light-bending. The tree's sweet fruit hung above him, each one worth a month's salary in off-world markets. He didn't reach for them. The Vethalians were known for hiding monitoring devices inside their most valuable resources.

Something felt wrong.

The sensation started as unease, then sharpened into certainty as Gavon extended his awareness through the tree. He expected carbon-based cellulose, water, trace minerals. Instead, his perception showed him chrominthium. The entire core of the tree, from roots to crown, had been replaced with the psychenetic metal.

He pulled his awareness back, but too late.

Energy pulsed from the tree—a wave of force that hammered through his skull and severed his connection to his Chrominthium Core. Gavon dropped to his knees, hands clutching his head as another pulse hit. Pain lanced behind his eyes, sharp and bright. He tried to activate his awareness, to bend the energy away or dampen its frequency, but nothing responded. The neural pathways between his conscious mind and the Chrominthium Core implanted in his brain had gone dark.

The pulses kept coming, each one driving him lower. His vision blurred. He couldn't keep his eyes open, couldn't think through the agony splitting his skull.

The ground shifted beneath him. A grinding sound, metal on stone, rose from below. Grass vanished, replaced by hard composite plating. The surface opened and Gavon fell.

He had maybe three seconds to process—darkness, the plate closing above, air rushing past. Then he hit bottom. Hard-packed dirt. Something cracked in his ribs. Soil cascaded down after him, filling his mouth, choking him.

"So the esteemed Gavon is trying to locate me." The voice came from somewhere in the darkness. Gavon recognized it immediately—Ilsidore. "We shall see how tough he really is. Has he earned the right to be Culminas's second in command?"

Gavon spat dirt and tried to stand. His awareness remained offline, useless. He reached for his wristchron—the emergency beacon built into his suit's interface—but a hand struck him across the face before his fingers reached the controls. He fell backwards, ribs screaming, and someone ripped the wristchron from his arm.

"This time you rely on natural abilities," Ilsidore said, his tone patronizing and amused. "Not the gifts the Order granted you."

Gavon struggled to rise. His lungs burned. Each breath brought less oxygen than the last. The air itself felt thin, or poisoned, or simply absent.

Light flared in the chamber's far corner. Five meters in diameter. Ilsidore stood near him, breathing apparatus covering his nose and mouth.

Gavon's vision darkened at the edges. He clawed for air that wouldn't come. The last thing he saw before losing consciousness was Ilsidore's face—staring at him with an intensity that held no recognition, no trace of the promising student he'd once trained.

✦ · · · ✦

Iona Jayden stood outside the Diplomatic Quarters, letting the breeze cool her skin. Before becoming a Shaper, she'd spent eight years as a planetologist, visiting worlds humans had never touched. Standing in an alien city built among living trees felt like coming home to something she'd sacrificed for the Order.

Lealvi spread out before her in vertical layers. Hardwood trees reached a hundred meters into the sky, their branches supporting suspended buildings where most Vethalians lived. Hover craft darted between the structures, following paths that seemed chaotic but probably made perfect sense to the locals. A few ground-level buildings housed off-worlders like herself—species that preferred horizontal architecture.

The breeze carried scents: tree sap, something floral she couldn't identify, ozone from the hover craft. She watched one vehicle land near the Quarters and disgorge three Vethalian females. They stood maybe a meter and a half tall, slight builds that suggested fragility. Iona knew better. She'd seen a Vethalian break a soldier's jaw with a single kick, an explosive burst of acrobatic violence that left the man unconscious before he hit the ground.

Rumors claimed the males lived underground, their minds linked into biological supercomputers that ran the vethalian fleet and designed their hybrid technologies. Iona had never seen one. Supposedly they were even smaller than the females, kept separate by choice—a willing sacrifice that vethalian culture revered. They'd given up autonomy to advance their species, and their people honored them for it. The thought still made her uncomfortable, but who was she to judge alien social structures built on different values?

One of the females noticed Iona watching and approached. Gray uniform, blue-green skin with ridge patterns swirling across her cheeks and forehead.

"My name is Cydel Irisynth." She extended her hand.

Iona took it, the grip firm despite Cydel's small frame. "You may call me Sharon Guildson." Her mission required the lie, and it came easily enough, but she hated giving it.

"May I buy you a drink?"

"That sounds wonderful." Cydel's eyes brightened with what might have been amusement. "We don't usually drink intoxicating liquids, preferring other substances, but it's been awhile since I experimented with your brew."

"Benjamin's Pub in an hour? I have business to attend to first."

"I'll see you then."

Cydel returned to her hover craft. Iona watched her leave, then turned her attention back to the Diplomatic Quarters. There were five compounds in this sector. She'd scanned three, found nothing unusual. Two more to check before meeting Cydel.

She hummed a tune that matched the rhythm of swaying branches and resumed her reconnaissance. The excitement of talking with a Vethalian later made the tedious scanning work almost pleasant.

+ · · · +

The drink tasted terrible—some local brew that Cydel claimed was popular—but Iona didn't complain. They talked for an hour, discussing music and art and the philosophical differences between species that evolved on high-gravity worlds versus low-gravity ones. Sharon Guildson, the persona Iona wore like uncomfortable clothing, laughed at appropriate moments and asked polite questions.

And Cydel knew she was lying the entire time.

✦ · · · ✦

Cydel left the pub and made her way toward the underground caverns where Sybil Muvere maintained her sanctum. Twenty standard minutes by hover craft, then another ten on foot through passages only Vethalians knew existed.

The entrance hatch required specific pheromones to open. Cydel released them—chemical keys coded to her biology—and the composite material peeled backward. She descended stairs carved from living rock, each step worn smooth by centuries of use.

Two guards met her at the first checkpoint. Sisters she recognized from training. She presented the mental password and the correct pheromone sequence. They let her pass without speaking.

The passage narrowed until Cydel had to turn sideways to squeeze through. Then it opened into a wide cavern spanning thirty meters across. A marble path stretched over a deep chasm, its surface inlaid with jewels in patterns that caught the phosphorescent light from fungus growing along the walls.

Cydel released another pheromone and stepped onto the path. Without the correct chemical signal, the fungus lining the chasm released poisonous spores. She'd seen the aftermath once—a Cabal spy who thought she could cross by holding her breath. The spores paralyzed her nervous system in seconds. She fell screaming into darkness.

Cydel quickened her pace. Three more caverns lay ahead, each one lit by different varieties of phosphorescent fungus. Ilmio blossoms grew in clusters near the passages, their scent bringing memories of home, the vethalian birthworld Volentril. Lealvi had these marble paths only where Sybils maintained their sanctums, but Volentril sparkled with them—thousands of jeweled walkways connecting the underground cities.

Cydel hesitated continuing in the third cavern. A presence lingered here, a fleeting impression on the psychic energy that all sentient beings left in their wake. Similar to a Shaper's signature, but altered. The resonance felt off.

She approached the final passage with her hand on her laser pistol. No guards at their posts. Across the chasm, the doors to the Symbiant Chambers stood open.

Her mind raced. How had someone gotten this far? The first checkpoint had been manned—she'd passed through normally. The pheromone locks on the marble pathways should have released poisonous spores at any intruder. Either the intruder had killed everyone between the entrance and here without leaving bodies, or they possessed capabilities that shouldn't exist. Neither possibility offered comfort.

Cydel crouched behind a stand of Ilmio blossoms and extended her psychic senses.

Daughter, you must hurry. The intruders have left.

Muvere's voice in her mind carried distress—an emotion Sybils rarely showed. Cydel had spoken with Muvere telepathically only once before, during her induction into the Candescent Sisterhood. The Sisterhoods discouraged casual use of psychic abilities, believing such powers should be reserved for necessity.

I will hurry, Mother.

Cydel sprinted across the passage. The fungus had been incinerated, the pheromone locks destroyed. She raised her laser pistol and extended her serrated blade, advancing toward the open doors with both weapons ready.

One of the sisters hung suspended in mid-air, arms and legs spread slightly from her body. No visible support. She wasn't moving—even her eyes remained fixed, locked on some distant point. Frozen in space like an insect in amber.

Further into the chamber, past six rows of symbiant pods, two more sisters had been fused with the technology. Their bodies protruded from the chrominthium surfaces, half-emerged as if they'd been pushed into solid metal. The fusion looked seamless. Molecular manipulation. A Shaper's work.

Fury and shame hit Cydel simultaneously. The Shaper she'd met—Sharon Guildson—had lied to her face. Smiled and drank terrible alcohol while her accomplices attacked the sanctum.

Yes, Cydel. It was a Shaper. But I believe a rogue one.

Cydel crossed the chamber to where Muvere lay in the back corner, dark green robes spread around her like a shroud. The Sybil's eyes remained closed. Her breathing came shallow and irregular.

Cydel knelt and placed a hand on Muvere's shoulder, strengthening their psychic connection. *Do I need to call for assistance?*

There is no need. The others are dead. I will soon follow them into the void.

The acceptance in Muvere's mental voice made Cydel's chest tighten. *What happened?*

That Shaper took something from me. Violated my psyche in ways I didn't know were possible. I feel myself unraveling. There were other vethalians with him. Ones from a Cabal. They helped him dismantle one of the pods.

Cydel stood and turned toward the rows of symbiant pods. Each one measured two meters in diameter, oval-shaped chrominthium shells with sensory nodes arranged along their ridges. Vethalian engineering at its finest—technology that let a trained sister project her consciousness across light-years, enter the minds of sentient beings, observe or even control them.

In the nearest row, one pod sat open and gutted. The sensory nodes had been removed. The internal chair where a sister would sit during melding was gone. Someone had taken the headset that connected users to dimensions beyond normal four-dimensional space.

The Shapers had their molecular awareness. The Vethalian sisterhoods had their symbiant chambers. Both groups shaped reality through different means and kept their true capabilities secret. Even the renegade Cabals understood the need for secrecy. If other species discovered that Vethalians could project into minds without consent, without detection—the consequences would be catastrophic.

Cydel moved to an intact pod and accessed its control panel. Using a symbiant chamber without Sybil permission carried severe punishment. But with Muvere dying and intruders stealing critical technology, Cydel had no time for proper authorization.

She typed a message on her datapad, alerting the other Sybils of the intrusion. Then she activated the pod.

During normal operations, another sister would manage the controls while Cydel entered the chamber. Now she'd have to operate it herself—a dangerous procedure that increased the risk of losing her consciousness in the spaces between dimensions.

The pod opened with a hydraulic hiss. Cydel holstered her pistol and pulled herself into the chair. The headset lowered onto her skull. She connected the thought nodes and pulled the internal control panel across her lap. A loud pop signaled the seal engaging. Cognition fluid began filling the chamber, surrounding her body.

Her perception shifted. The pod's interior faded as her consciousness moved into another dimension. This transition killed some newly inducted sisters—their minds unable to navigate the dimensional shift, leaving them catatonic.

Cydel concentrated, extending her psyche in search of the Shaper who'd called herself Sharon Guildson. The presence appeared quickly—not as strong as the rogue Shaper's twisted signature, but stronger than an unaugmented human's.

She didn't want to take control of the Shaper's body. Even attempting that would trigger resistance, alert the target immediately. Better to interject a thought, a warning, make it seem like the Shaper's own realization.

Cydel cleared her mind and prepared the projection. Rushing this part led to catastrophic failures—consciousness scattered across dimensions, unable to find its way home.

She reached out and touched the Shaper's mind, ready to deliver her warning about the rogue Shaper who'd stolen symbiant technology and left sisters dead in his wake.

✛ · · · ✛

Gavon woke bound to a chair.

His arms had been secured to armrests carved from polished Chrominthium—or something made to look like it. Blue-tinted silver. If genuine, the five chairs in this windowless room represented enough wealth to buy a governorship on a moderately populated world.

The other four chairs held aliens. A Novrin, a Grevax, a Vethalian, and an Omatrin. Gavon didn't recognize any of them. But he recognized what had been done to them—the backs of their heads cut open, wires dangling from the incisions and spliced together before running to a central terminal.

He tried to turn his awareness on to examine his own skull. Nothing. The same dead emptiness he'd felt in the underground chamber. He twisted his head as far as the restraints allowed and saw wires trailing from his chair toward the terminal, confirming his worst fear.

Ilsidore had opened his head. Accessed his Chrominthium Core directly.

Shapers rarely survived Core removal. The implantation process alone killed ten percent of initiates. Extraction—even performed by expert biotechnicians on Endrunel—left most subjects in vegetative states.

"Ahh, I see the other Shaper has awakened." The Novrin spoke in the high, nasal pitch his species used for human languages. Avian and reptilian features combined unpleasantly on his face. "What happened? Did you do something to upset him? I can understand if he's a xenophobe wanting to take his ire out on us. But on one of his own kind?"

Gavon grimaced and said nothing. Novrin were known for antagonistic speech, particularly toward humans. Their talons could shred human skin effortlessly. Only the best-trained soldiers survived hand-to-hand combat with them.

"You know, he must not have a clue why he's bound and operated on like us," the Vethalian woman said from beyond the Novrin. "No Shaper would allow another to take out their Chrominthium Core like the other has done."

Panic tried to surface. Gavon pushed it down. He'd trained for crisis situations, learned to function under extreme stress. But this—having his Core accessed, his awareness offline, strapped to a chair in an unknown location—pushed him closer to the edge than any mission he'd undertaken.

Soft blue lights activated in the room's four corners. The harsh white central light shut off. A door opened behind them—Gavon caught movement in his peripheral vision but couldn't turn far enough to see.

Two Vethalians entered and checked the incisions in each captive's skull. They worked quickly, efficiently, then departed.

Ilsidore entered.

He wore a standard Shaper uniform, identical to Gavon's except for a small interface patch on his chest. Gavon had never seen that configuration before. Ilsidore moved past each chair, studying the occupants, saving Gavon for last.

He bent close, meeting Gavon's eyes. "I remember you being a kind instructor. Patient, unlike others at the academy." He straightened. "It's a shame this may kill you." He looked at the Novrin, who had a mischievous expression on his face. "You might find this amusing, but he has a better chance of surviving than you."

The Novrin laughed and shrugged as if he couldn't care less.

"What is all of this?" Gavon kept his voice steady despite the rage building in his chest. If any of these four escaped and reported what a Shaper had done to them, the Order would face severe consequences. The Vethalians were humanity's closest allies. The Grevax remained mysterious, the Omatrin mercenary, and the Novrin neutral—watching other species with inscrutable motivations. But this act of violence would turn them all against the Order.

"This," Ilsidore said, pacing and gesturing at the wires on the ground, "is the key to the cosmos." He stopped, turned to face them. "Your infamous leader, Culminas, didn't prove anything after the Last Wars. Yes, he discovered Chrominthium and built the first psychenetic accelerators. But it was much like a toddler taking his first steps. There is so much more out there to discover, and this...if you can handle it...will show you."

He crossed between the chairs toward the door. "Rest as best you can. Later, after I finish making adjustments in the other room, the five of you will be put to the test. Then I'll join you."

The door closed. Panels opened in the walls and small medical drones floated into the room. The first one reached Gavon and injected something into his neck. He tried to fight the spreading drowsiness, using molecular awareness to neutralize the drug. But his Core wasn't functioning properly. His abilities remained dormant. He could only struggle briefly before consciousness faded again.

✦ · · · ✦

Iona stood in front of the communications panel in her quarters and couldn't make herself activate it.

Gavon had been missing for eight hours. Her partner Exen Rual waited with twenty other Shapers at an outpost on Lealvi's nearest moon. One transmission would bring them all down. But something—intuition, instinct, whatever unscientific impulse she wanted to name it—warned her that breaking communication silence would be disastrous.

As a planetologist, Iona didn't trust gut feelings. Her Shaper abilities seemed supernatural to outsiders, but they were based on science and logic. Molecular awareness, dimensional physics, the proven mathematics of string law. Nothing mystical about any of it.

Still, she hesitated.

Gavon had given explicit orders. Maintain silence unless the diplomatic mission failed. He'd been secretive about the real objective, providing only the cover story about security detail for the ambassador. Iona had assumed he had good reasons for compartmentalization.

Now she wondered if he'd gone after something alone.

She sat at the ornate desk—its surface designed to mimic the color patterns of leaves she'd seen swaying in Lealvi's trees. Her datapad activated automatically. She pulled up Gavon's last known coordinates and began analyzing the terrain.

Sharon. Do not be alarmed.

Iona rose from her chair and slipped into her molecular awareness. A full scan of the room showed nothing—no hidden devices, no transmitters. She had no implants someone could hack remotely. Yet the voice had spoken directly into her mind.

It is Cydel Irisynth, the Vethalian you met earlier.

Iona's awareness stayed active, searching for threats. *Why are you talking to me like this?*

I will explain later. But one of your kind has gone rogue, and another is in trouble. I have found his location and will project the exact coordinates once I have converted the data.

What kind of trouble?

Iona released her awareness, conserving power.

That I do not know. But the rogue Shaper has hired some of our adversaries to sabotage us and is altering the psyche around him in an unusual way. I will send the coordinates to your datapad and will be there when you arrive.

How do I know this isn't a setup?

Iona knew Vethalian society had fractures—sisterhoods that governed openly, cabals that worked against them. If Cydel belonged to a cabal, this could be an elaborate trap.

Those who would like to see you fail on Lealvi do not have the ability to talk like this.

I will be at the coordinates you sent me. And my name is not Sharon Guildson but Iona Jayden, a Shaper of the Order of Infinity.

Iona checked her grav disc, made sure her meld dagger components were secure in her suit's storage. Everything Cydel said made sense. Gavon hadn't shared the mission details because he was hunting a rogue Shaper. The Order never advertised when members defected. Too much political damage.

More than once, factions had petitioned to outlaw the Order entirely. If a rogue Shaper had discovered some new technique, some untested way to manipulate matter, Iona needed to act fast.

She walked down the corridor toward the garage where she'd parked the hover car she'd used for earlier reconnaissance. As she moved, she debated contacting the rest of the void contingency. But Gavon had given explicit orders.

She decided to trust him.

The hover car's doors opened vertically as she approached. It had a sleek design common in this sector, with a dark gray exterior and matching interior. She plugged Cydel's coordinates into the nav computer and set the maximum speed that wouldn't trigger automated alerts.

She had fifteen minutes to destination. She spent the time scanning her datapad for anomalies, searching for anything that might explain what the rogue Shaper was trying to accomplish on Lealvi.

✦ · • · ✦

Gavon fought to stay awake, but exhaustion dragged him down repeatedly.

Each time he slept, the same dream consumed him. Drifting in hyperspace without a vessel, somehow alive and sane. Moving past the fifth and sixth dimensions into the seventh. There he existed as something close to a deity—altering worlds with thoughts, needing no Chrominthium Core to reshape reality.

The dream repeated with disturbing consistency. The other four captives seemed trapped in the same experience. The Novrin laughed and snorted every few minutes while unconscious.

More than disturbing, the dream felt illicit. Like tapping into knowledge he shouldn't possess. And it was exhausting. The sleep brought no rest, only increasingly drained him.

Gavon used every scrap of willpower to remain awake while the others drifted. He thought about advanced lessons from Culminas—particularly the one where Culminas had demonstrated removing his Chrominthium Core and using ambient kinetic energy to activate molecular awareness. The technique resembled these dream sequences. But Culminas had warned against exploring the seventh dimension before mastering the fifth and sixth.

The fifth and sixth dimensions allowed Shapers to "translate" void spheres across the universe faster than light. They enabled molecular awareness to function in standard four-dimensional space.

The seventh dimension remained theoretical. Dangerous and unexplored.

"I wouldn't try doing that, Gavon." Ilsidore's voice came through a speaker behind the chairs. Gavon sat up straighter, forcing defiance into his posture. "In your condition, with how I have you connected to my interdimensional psyche accelerator, if you tried to activate your awareness, you'll fry your gray matter in an instant."

"Why are you doing this?" Gavon kept his voice quiet but firm. His head ached from the effort of staying conscious. He'd never felt this weak.

"I am doing what your Culminas cannot. He is a weak individual, afraid of unleashing his full potential. Why do you think we evolved from apes? To continue living in ignorance, looking to the heavens for answers? I think not."

"Culminas has his reasons. He still thinks he may have made a mistake with his discovery and actions in forming the Order."

The Novrin and Vethalian were awake now, listening. The Omatrin looked co-matose, and the Grevax's clawed hands twitched rhythmically.

"His reasons are only to have control over people like you. Those who follow him faithfully without much thought." The door opened. Ilsidore entered and moved to stand near Gavon. "But you are not the type to just be a follower, Gavon. I know what you have been experiencing in what you think are dreams. Unlike the others here, you've come close to understanding. In fact, none of the others have come close like you."

He moved to the Novrin and drew a utility combat knife from his suit. One quick motion across the Novrin's throat. Blood gushed out, running down the creature's chest to pool on the floor. The Novrin's eyes widened briefly. It let out another round of peculiar chuckles before dying.

Ilsidore killed the Omatrin and Grevax with the same efficiency, showing no hesitation. Then he paused in front of the Vethalian.

"You are too beautiful to waste like that." He leaned close and kissed the Vethalian's cheek. She showed disgust, her eyes narrowing. Ilsidore laughed. "Don't worry, I was referring to your intellect. I have always been fascinated by your kind and your Symbiant Chambers. You are not cattle like the other two."

The Vethalian women who'd worked for Ilsidore earlier entered and removed the three corpses one at a time. After clearing the room, they left.

Ilsidore paced in front of Gavon and the surviving Vethalian, hands behind his back. "I think tomorrow we will achieve what I have set out to do. To influence hyperspace and transfer our consciousness permanently."

He exited. The door sealed behind him.

Gavon didn't like anything about what he'd heard. Ilsidore had definitely lost his mind. This technique he described—Gavon had never heard of it. He'd only seen Shapers lose their minds trying to go beyond what Culminas taught. Even attempting to activate molecular awareness for the first time put initiates at risk of destroying their minds or trapping them in altered consciousness states.

Drowsiness pulled at him again. This time Gavon didn't fight it. If he wasn't dreaming—if this interdimensional psychenetic accelerator actually connected him to something real—then there had to be a way through it to attack Ilsidore's psyche.

Gavon had more experience than his former student, despite Ilsidore's talent. He was known for ingenuity. He would find a way to stop Ilsidore and protect the Order from further disasters.

He let the darkness take him, preparing to fight back through whatever dimension Ilsidore had opened.

+ · · · +

Iona brought the hover car down near the coordinates and spotted Cydel standing beside a lone Ilmio tree. The Vethalian wore a light gray combat suit and carried a flechette pistol. Iona ran a final scan for heat signatures, found nothing suspicious, and landed.

She stepped out and joined Cydel near the tree. Cydel pointed at disturbed earth and grass. Iona activated her molecular awareness and saw the outline of a retractable grate leading to a tunnel entrance. She extended her awareness into the locking mechanism, altered the molecular bonds holding it closed, and slid the grate back.

The tunnel dropped five meters into darkness. Iona's awareness mapped it completely—dimensions, surface texture, structural composition.

"The drop isn't far," she whispered.

Cydel nodded. Both crouched low and dropped into the tunnel. Cydel landed gracefully, rolling into a defensive stance with her pistol raised. Iona created an updraft at the last moment, slowing her descent and displacing the inertia so her landing made no sound.

The smell hit her immediately. Death and decay. A Novrin corpse lay in the corner, throat cut, eyes eaten by scavengers. This didn't match Vethalian construction standards. They built humane deterrent systems, never allowing vermin into their structures. And Lealvi's wilderness provided ample food—no reason for scavengers to enter buildings.

Cydel crossed toward an opening that led into a hallway. A Vethalian dropped from the ceiling and lunged at her. Cydel feinted left, kicked her attacker in the side of the head with her right foot, and fired two flechette rounds. The attacker skidded across the floor to land near the Novrin corpse.

Three more Vethalians entered, all wearing dark green combat suits—Inquest Cabal uniforms. They carried sonic pulse rifles.

Iona pulled her grav-disc with her left hand. Her meld dagger's components flowed from storage in her right arm, assembling in her palm. She threw the grav disc into the air and broke it into thousands of small projectiles, directing them toward the attackers. Two dodged to the sides. The third hesitated—projectiles ripped through her body. Blood seeped from dozens of wounds.

Iona extended her awareness, pulling the projectiles back in an arc to the right. They caught another attacker as she tried to find cover. The pieces coalesced back into a disc and hit the final target in the neck, decapitating her.

The last Vethalian fired her sonic pulse rifle at both of them, then threw a flash grenade while retreating past Cydel into the hallway. She kept firing. Iona used her awareness to deflect a round that would have hit Cydel in the chest.

Cydel rushed to the hallway entrance and fired her pistol three times. The last attacker's rifle clattered to the ground as she slumped against the wall.

"Knowing how the Cabal operates," Cydel said as she inspected the body, "whoever purchased their services will already know we're here. They'll send more to cover their tracks. We must hurry."

She continued down the hallway. Iona returned her grav disc to its holster and followed, preparing herself for whatever they'd find deeper in this facility.

The hallway terminated at a reinforced door. Iona scanned it with her awareness—layered chrominthium circuits designed to alert Ilsidore the moment she began manipulation. She looked at Cydel and shook her head.

"He'll know we're coming the second I touch this."

"Then we go fast." Cydel raised her flechette pistol and stepped back.

Iona focused her awareness on the door's molecular structure, found the weakest points in the metal composite, and sheared through them in three precise cuts. The door fell inward with a heavy crash. They moved through—Cydel swept right along the wall, Iona took the left.

✦ · · · ✦

The room beyond stretched ten meters across, circular, with two chairs remaining from what had clearly been five. Gavon sat in one chair, head tilted forward, wires trailing from the back of his skull to a central terminal. Dried blood crusted on his neck. A Vethalian woman Iona didn't recognize occupied the other chair, similarly restrained and wired.

Ilsidore stood at the terminal, fingers moving across a holographic interface. He didn't turn when they entered.

"Iona Jayden." His voice held casual recognition. "The planetologist. I've reviewed your work since joining the Order. Competent applications of molecular awareness, but you still think in terms of classification and analysis rather than true manipulation."

Iona moved into the room, awareness extended and searching for traps. "Release Gavon. Now."

"Gavon is participating in the most significant experiment in human history." Ilsidore turned to face them. Something about the space around him looked wrong—air distorted, reality bent slightly in his presence. "Soon, he and I will permanently transfer our consciousness into the seventh dimension. We'll exist as pure awareness, able to manipulate matter across the universe without the crude limitations of these meat shells."

"You're insane," Cydel said. She'd moved to flank Ilsidore, pistol trained on his chest.

"Insane?" Ilsidore smiled. "The Shapers manipulate molecules. Your Sybils project consciousness across light-years. But both are children playing with toys compared to what I've achieved. The seventh dimension, Iona. Culminas is too afraid to explore it, but I'm not."

Iona reached toward Gavon's restraints with her awareness, intending to sever them. Agony lanced through her skull the moment she extended toward the chair. She staggered, vision blurring. Through watering eyes she saw Ilsidore watching with detached curiosity.

"The interdimensional field around the apparatus," he said. "It feeds on molecular awareness, uses it as fuel. The more you try to manipulate matter within its range, the more it drains you. Fascinating effect. I discovered it by accident during the prototype phase."

Cydel fired. Three flechette rounds crossed the distance in a fraction of a second. Ilsidore raised his hand and the rounds stopped mid-air—suspended, frozen completely. Not slowed but stopped.

"Crude projectiles." He closed his fist and the rounds crumpled like paper. "My awareness already operates across multiple dimensional layers. Physical momentum means nothing when you can redirect kinetic vectors at their source."

Iona assessed their options. Without her awareness, she was just a woman with a knife. Cydel had other weapons, but if Ilsidore could stop flechettes mid-flight, nothing conventional would work.

Ilsidore turned back to his terminal. "I suggest you leave before the cascade begins. The dimensional bleed will be unpleasant for unprotected consciousness in the immediate vicinity."

Gavon's head jerked up. His eyes focused on Iona with desperate intensity. His mouth moved but produced no sound. She stepped closer despite the dull throb building in her head from proximity to the field.

"Gavon..."

"You cannot help him," Ilsidore said without turning. "He's already halfway into the seventh dimension. Soon the transition will be irreversible."

A sound came from behind them—low, warbling, resonating uncomfortably in Iona's bones. She turned and saw air rippling near the doorway. A shape formed, translucent at first, then gaining substance. Vaguely humanoid but stretched along axes that didn't correspond to height, width, or depth—elongated in directions that shouldn't exist in three-dimensional space.

Cydel gasped. "Mother Muvere."

The shape flickered, losing cohesion. Muvere's form wavered like static, threatening to dissipate entirely.

Cydel. I cannot... maintain... The psychic voice fractured, breaking apart.

Cydel's eyes widened. She pressed both hands to her temples, face contorted in concentration. "I'm anchoring you. Use my consciousness as a tether."

The Vethalian's body went rigid, trembling with effort. Blood trickled from her nose. Iona saw what was happening—Cydel was projecting her own psychic presence outward, giving Muvere something to stabilize against. It was the same principle as the Symbiant Chambers, but raw, unprotected, dangerous.

Muvere's form solidified slightly, gaining definition. Her robes flowed like liquid. Her face flickered between solid and transparent. When she spoke, the words bypassed ears entirely, forming directly in Iona's mind.

He severed my body's connection to my projected consciousness. Ripped through the dimensional membrane while I was mid-projection. He assumed that would kill the psyche itself.

Ilsidore spun from his terminal. For the first time, Iona saw surprise on his face. "Impossible. I severed your connection. You should be..."

Dead? Muvere's psychic voice sharpened. *A projection without an anchor point, clinging to coherence out of desperation? You're half right. My body is gone. But my consciousness remained caught in the sixth dimensional layer—and you opened a door to the seventh. You wanted to prove consciousness survives physical death. Congratulations.*

Muvere's form shifted, closing the distance faster than Iona could track. Ilsidore raised his hand, space warping around it, but Muvere's hand passed through his defenses as if they weren't there.

Muvere's hand touched Ilsidore's forehead.

He screamed—pure terror that cut off abruptly as his body went rigid. His eyes remained open but empty, staring at nothing. The distortion in the air around him intensified, becoming a visible spiral of warped space that contracted inward, focusing on the point where Muvere touched him.

You wanted access to the seventh dimensional layer. Let me show you what exists there.

Ilsidore's body convulsed. His mouth moved but produced no sound. His hands clawed at nothing. Iona felt a pulling sensation—not gravity, but something pulling at the space her awareness occupied. She grabbed the wall to steady herself. Cydel dropped to one knee, both hands pressed to her head, still maintaining her anchor for Muvere despite the strain.

There are consciousnesses in the seventh layer. Structures of awareness that evolved—or were constructed—without physical origin. They recognize intrusions. They respond to them.

Gavon's eyes snapped open fully. Despite the wires still connected to his skull, despite the pain, he activated his molecular awareness. Not to escape but to attack.

He couldn't reach Ilsidore physically, but they were connected through the inter-dimensional apparatus. Gavon pushed his consciousness along that connection, not trying to fight the pull of the seventh dimension but joining it, adding his weight to what Muvere was doing.

"Gavon, no..." Iona started forward.

Gavon's body convulsed in the chair. Blood ran from his ears. But his aware-ness—trained, disciplined, honed by Culminas—added structure to Muvere's attack. Where she pulled Ilsidore toward the consciousness structures, Gavon prevented him from pulling back. A trap with two jaws instead of one.

I am delivering you to them, Ilsidore. Your consciousness will remain locked in that dimensional space while your body continues its autonomic functions, empty.

The warped space collapsed inward with a sound like reality cracking—sharp and crystalline, as if the fundamental structure of space itself was fracturing. Ilsidore's scream resumed for a fraction of a second—then silence. His body remained standing, perfectly still, eyes vacant. He breathed, but nothing else moved. Just a shell.

Muvere's form flickered, growing more transparent. The consciousness structures in the seventh layer had noticed her interference. Iona could see it happening—threads of something reaching through Muvere's projection, pulling at her.

Cydel. Daughter. I cannot maintain this state. They are... claiming me as well. The price for delivering Ilsidore. Tell the Sisterhood... the seventh dimension is not empty. There are things there that should not be disturbed. Remember...

The Sybil dissipated like smoke—but not naturally. Pulled apart, drawn into the same space where Ilsidore had gone.

Cydel's hands dropped from her temples. She swayed, nearly collapsing. Temperature stabilized. Iona found she could breathe normally. The interdimensional field had collapsed the moment Ilsidore's consciousness was severed from his body. Without his awareness powering it, the apparatus was just inert machinery.

Ilsidore's body stood motionless for three more seconds. Then it collapsed like a puppet with cut strings, crumpling to the floor in an awkward heap.

Cydel crossed the room unsteadily and knelt beside the shell. She placed two fingers against his neck, then looked up at Iona. "Pulse is present. Breathing is autonomous. But there is no psychic presence. Nothing. Just biological processes continuing without consciousness."

Iona moved to Gavon's chair, examining the apparatus with her awareness now that the field had collapsed. The wires threaded through his Chrominthium Core's interface ports—brutal surgery, but not immediately fatal. She began disconnecting them, one at a time.

"Gavon. Can you hear me?"

His eyes focused on her slowly. For a moment he just looked at her, and she saw something in his expression—gratitude, exhaustion, and deep sorrow.

"You came," he said simply.

"Of course I did." She helped him stand. "You're my friend."

"I trained him, Iona. Ilsidore was my student. I should have seen..."

"Not now. We'll process this later. Right now we need to get you out of here."

He nodded, then his expression shifted as memory returned. "I saw it. The seventh dimensional layer. Muvere was right...there are consciousness structures there." He shuddered. "They don't process information sequentially. They exist across multiple states simultaneously. When Ilsidore's consciousness touched them..." He paused, swallowing. "They didn't devour him. They integrated him. He's part of their structure now, experiencing every moment of his existence simultaneously, forever. No linear time. No escape. Just... eternal present."

The concept disturbed her on a fundamental level. "That's..."

"Worse than death," Gavon finished. "Much worse. He wanted to become a god. Instead he became a component in something incomprehensible."

Iona freed the last connection and helped Gavon maintain his balance. "We need to get you medical attention. And we need to contact Culminas."

"The Vethalian," Gavon said, gesturing weakly toward the other chair.

Cydel was already there, carefully removing the wires from the captive sister's head. The woman's eyes opened, unfocused but aware.

"Can you walk?" Cydel asked.

The Vethalian nodded shakily. "I think so."

Behind them, Ilsidore's body lay motionless on the floor—an empty shell abandoned by its consciousness. Iona looked at it and felt no satisfaction, only unease. They'd stopped him, but the cost had been Muvere's existence and the discovery that something waited in dimensions beyond their understanding. Something that responded to intrusion with absolute, incomprehensible consequence.

"Let's move," Iona said. "We need to secure this facility and make sure no one else tries to replicate his work."

Gavon straightened slightly, finding his balance. "Culminas needs to know. The seventh dimensional layer isn't unexplored because we haven't tried. It's unexplored because conscious interaction with what exists there produces psychic trauma. Or worse...permanent dissociation."

They left the chamber together, supporting Gavon and the rescued Vethalian between them. Behind them, in the silence, Ilsidore's shell remained motionless on the cold floor—a warning carved in flesh of the price for reaching too far into realms beyond human comprehension.

Steed of Destiny

Below, the jungle planet spread like a green curse as Illmar eased his cruiser into the clearing on Jilarska. Miles of impenetrable vegetation stretched in every direction—animals that wanted nothing more than to devour him, and sometimes worse depending on which planet he worked. That strange beetle boring into his testicles flashed through his memory. The burning sensation had lasted even after the nurse removed it. He'd kept the beetle preserved in a container on his cruiser, ready to share the story with any lucky passenger he brought aboard.

Industrial worlds were so much better. The food was greasy, the drinks hit hard, and the women... The local women on jungle planets would try to do more than give him a good time and drain his hard-earned funds.

"Who the fuck are you mate?" A skinny native stepped forward as Illmar departed his cruiser onto the clearing marked with burn scars from other craft landings. His cruiser always drew stares—bright neon orange with multi-colored lights on the prow, rotating between lightshows he'd created. The pride swelled in his chest. He made sure to tell whoever would listen when he visited the pubs and eateries on starports.

"None of your business." Illmar began his stare-down with the native, then let it go. Still recovering from the night before. "You can call me Illmar. Most local authorities call me other things."

"Illmar, hmm." The native looked him up and down with judgment. A human male, too skinny for Illmar's taste—he himself was bulky even for someone who was 6'2". The native wore a beret with matching camo shirt and pants, carrying only a projectile rifle, stun net, and canteen. "They call me Ligee. I'm a guide for hire. Are you here after that

Grevax monstrosity? You should have seen the last fellow who tried to capture him, whoo boy."

"Well, I'm not a boy." Illmar poked out his chest. His camo tank top and black dungarees felt right for the hunt. Long curly sandy hair pulled back in a ponytail, vintage aviator sunglasses resting on his head. The M-607 pulse rifle with sling on his right shoulder, the Thorsen fusion hand cannon in his utility belt holster. The hand cannon was usually overkill but subtlety had never been his style. Best to leave a calling card if a mercenary wanted preference finding another job. "You're hired, if you like a strong drink afterwards, and not more than 5% of the bonus."

"8% and then you have a deal. You can keep the strong drink."

"7% and at least one shot of top shelf."

"Done. Follow me. The beast is less than a mile away, I've been tracking him... It." Ligee pointed at his wristchron, that wide grin spreading across his face. "I'll upload my resume to your aug if you need. Plenty of satisfied customers."

"No augs here," Illmar replied, falling into step behind Ligee. "And if you're not being honest, there's always Lucy." He patted the butt of the hand cannon. He didn't usually name his weapons, but this one had a special place in his heart. "Just show me the way so we can get paid."

The jungle seemed to stretch the mile into something endless. Trees towered over them—too many different species he didn't recognize or care to remember from previous excursions. The underbrush annoyed him, especially the knee-high plants with berries that burst as they passed. Ligee warned him to be careful not to accidentally transfer any residue to his mouth.

After another half-mile, the trees and underbrush thickened, slowing their pace until they reached another clearing. The air hung thick and Illmar drank from his canteen. The smell of rotten flesh hit him strong, and as they continued moving, he saw a clearing similar to his landing site ahead. Instead of burn marks from ships, a troop of ape-like creatures lay decimated on one of the grassy knolls. Nothing stirred—only half-eaten flesh and bones remained. In the shadows of the treeline, a pair of dark purple eyes belonged to a bulky figure he couldn't quite make out.

At the jungle's edge, Ligee crouched low and motioned for Illmar to do the same. He quietly typed on his wristchron: *It is up ahead. Not sure if it will flee or attack you when you approach.*

Illmar crept along the left side of the jungle edge, bringing his pulse rifle around. The Grevax creature strolled toward the piles of bone and flesh on four legs at the bottom of its torso, while the other two on its upper torso brought up pieces for inspection. After tasting the half-rotten flesh, it let out a loud bellow that echoed around them—deep and guttural, unpleasant to his ears.

Through the scope of his pulse rifle, Illmar took aim. It fit the description from the bounty data he'd downloaded to his ship from the office near Torafa's Grill. Six limbs total—four for travel, two for manipulating items. Hide harder than a rhino's ass, face uglier than a vulture's. If he got close, there'd be the telltale smell of sulfur, and the readout had said its bite was possibly venomous.

Even after humanity had left Earth millennia ago, several organizations still used creatures and items from there as reference points. Maybe one day when he retired he'd try to make the pilgrimage back to his people's birthworld. First though, he needed to capture this beast and collect his reward.

The Grevax put down the bone it had been gnawing and focused on Illmar as he tried to approach cautiously. He'd borrowed an extra stun net from Ligee—after placing a couple of pulse rounds on its hindquarters and closing in, he'd throw the net. He hadn't had much training with weapons like nets, but he was a natural. Except when still under the effects from late night escapades, his hand-eye coordination was phenomenal.

The Grevax had other plans and began laying low, winding up like a spring. It opened its mouth and Illmar could see yellowish-green liquid on its long sharp teeth.

"That beast is poisonous. Fucking hell." He couldn't see Ligee anymore but thought he heard someone laughing in the distance back where he'd come from.

Closing its mouth, it charged toward Illmar. Despite its size—over seven feet in height when standing—the Grevax was surprisingly fast. Illmar missed with his first shot, hitting the ground nearby and showering dirt, bone fragments, and rotten flesh into the air. The next two hit their mark, tagging the beast in chest and head.

The shots slowed the Grevax only slightly. Illmar rolled to his right, narrowly missing its charge. It turned around and Illmar already had his pulse rifle trained on it. The Grevax was injured by his well-placed shots—nothing critical, but its pace was sluggish and one clawed hand held where he'd hit it on the head.

"Meeeeeaat," the Grevax said in a barely distinguishable tone, but Illmar got the gist of its intentions.

"Damn, we have something in common, but I'd rather have pork than human or your kind." He fired three more rounds. One badly damaged the left front leg, the other two grazed the grevax's sides. He didn't want to take chances since this Grevax was more intelligent than the bounty file had indicated.

The Grevax crouched again as Illmar approached with the stun net. He shouldered his pulse rifle and threw the net toward it. At the last second, the Grevax rolled out of the way and pounced on Illmar. It pinned him, spreading out its limbs and leaning over him slowly while opening its maw.

Illmar tried to push the beast off him. Even with adrenaline kicking in and the creature wounded, it was too much to handle. Only his right arm was free, and with his pulse rifle underneath him, he'd have to try the hand cannon. He slowly moved his hand toward it, not wanting to attract attention.

As he palmed his hand cannon and looked up at the Grevax getting dangerously close with those venomous teeth, he heard the release of pressure. The Grevax reached up to a dart now sticking out of its neck and slowly fell next to Illmar, resting on its side. Illmar sprang to his knees, but before he could aim his hand cannon toward where he thought the initial round came from, the same rush of air stung him in the center of his chest. He dropped his hand cannon and tried to pull out the dart, but felt his strength draining.

Out of the nearby treeline, Ligee approached with a tranquilizer rifle resting in the crook of his left arm and that same wide grin.

"Should have asked for my resume," Ligee said, standing next to Illmar. "If you had a military grade aug, you might have been able to detect that I was full of shit."

Illmar tried to reach for his fallen hand cannon but dropped to the ground instead. "I should have known. Who in hell calls their child Ligee? Lame..." He tried to fight unconsciousness but it was no use. Ligee pressed his wristchron and off in the distance, a small ship approached over the jungle canopy.

✦ · · ✦

Illmar opened his eyes and tried to stand from where he lay. Still groggy from the tranquilizer, after several tries he managed to sit up. The room was dim, only lit by a nearby panel across from the set of bars he was behind. The other three sides were plascrete walls—a makeshift cell. There wasn't an outline of a door or locking mechanism on the bars.

"So you're awake now," Ligee said from somewhere distant. Illmar couldn't tell if his voice came from a speaker or around the corner. All he knew was if Ligee released him from this chamber, he'd show that jungle worlder it wasn't wise to restrain him. He'd done his time in lockup and was skilled at escaping situations like this, especially when sober.

"I am awake. Why don't you show your ugly face?" Illmar stood and grabbed the bars. Ligee casually strolled into view, not bothering to look at him, instead focusing on readouts on the panel.

"No need for unpleasantries like that, Illmar. I'm only here for profit like you. Besides, after the Grevax is in the hands of the Biosphere Conglomerate, I might let you live, if you give me the codes to your cruiser."

"Never. Do what you have to, but that's my baby. I'd rather rot than see you enjoy her." Illmar released his grip and stood back. A loud bellow echoed throughout the bay they were in. The Grevax had to be in another cell like his, waking up to the same reality. "Good luck trying to offload that thing."

Ligee shrugged, glancing at Illmar as he walked out of view. Illmar fumed and began thinking how he could surprise Ligee when he opened his cage. He was a mercenary roaming the stars looking for work, but as a young man, he'd served his time in the local militia. The Giyan militia had selected him for advanced training. He'd never forget his Covert Resilience and Extraction Training. Six months in CRET had almost broken him, but unknown to his commanders, it made him one of the best mercenaries this side of the galaxy. He sat back down on the cold hard floor and welcomed the vibration of the engine he felt.

✦ · · · ✦

"Put these on," Ligee said, handing restraining cuffs through the bars. He'd changed from camo into a dark blue business suit. Illmar wondered why he was dressed like that. The Biosphere Conglomerate didn't care much for outsiders, only here for the precious Grevax biodata that was hard to come by.

The bars retracted and Ligee pointed a laser pistol at Illmar, motioning for him to walk in front. Illmar saw his chance. As he passed Ligee, he dropped to his hands and swept his legs behind him. Ligee jumped over them and fired at Illmar. The blast narrowly missed, but Illmar managed to turn around and wrap his arms around Ligee. He head-butted him and let go with his wrists, kneeing him in the chest. Ligee fell backward and looked shocked as Illmar stood over him.

"You should have investigated who I was. Even though your augs are probably after-market trash, they would have given you information about who I am." Illmar kicked him again and bent over to take Ligee's wristchron. He found the controls to the restraints and released them, throwing them at Ligee, causing him to yell. Illmar turned in the opposite direction toward a narrow corridor leading to a hatch and moved quickly through it.

Before him in another bay was a similar cell, only slightly larger. The Grevax was there, standing on all fours. It looked curiously at Illmar, then over at a panel on the wall. The lighting was better in this bay. A bay door was open on the other end with a ramp extending down toward a concrete pad. Ligee must have had these cells constructed in the cargo bay—not the traditional setup slavers or bounty hunters used. Illmar was glad about that. Those were harder to escape from.

At the panel, there was no passcode needed to access the bar controls. He figured out how to release the Grevax, taking a risk but assuming the creature was intelligent enough to understand they were both in the same situation. The bars retracted upward and the Grevax bolted in his direction. Illmar sidestepped, but as he turned to react, he saw he wasn't its target. Ligee had limped into the room and the Grevax knocked him over.

"Meeeeeaat," the Grevax said slowly, as if about to enjoy its favorite meal. Illmar looked away as a guttural howl came from Ligee. The sound of flesh and bones crunching echoed through the bay. Even though Ligee probably deserved what was happening, Illmar didn't want to be part of it and left back through the corridor to find the cockpit.

Through another corridor in the opposite direction from his cell, he found a hatch and opened it. Inside was the cockpit—similar round design to most but sterile, as if Ligee belonged to a military organization that performed routine inspections. Illmar found this boring. What was the purpose of piloting a ship across the wonders of the universe if the pilot couldn't add their own effects?

Sitting in the first chair of the front row, Illmar brought up the control panel from the chair's side. He tried to access the controls to no avail. Ligee must have set up a hidden bioscanner he couldn't find, and even if he found it, there wouldn't be much of Ligee left after the Grevax finished.

Out of the corner of his eye, he noticed movement on the only display screen that was on. Focusing on it, Illmar saw black-clad individuals walking down an exit ramp from a nearby ship bearing the green and silver Biosphere Conglomerate logo. Four in total, cautiously making their way toward Ligee's ship in the black scrubs their biotechnicians wore before performing operations. Unfortunately, a fifth exited their ship—one of their agents. Illmar had heard about these. They weren't different from most factions' covert operatives except they were humans enhanced by other alien DNA at birth.

This agent wore a silver flight suit and had an extra set of arms. Instead of hands, there were razor-sharp talons and other pointed barbs along the forearms. In all his travels, he'd never seen any known sapient species with arms like the agent's. It was probably from one of the many genetic experiments the Grevax performed on their own kind, added to the agent when he was a fetus. There had to be something different about the Grevax currently in the cargo bay for the detail the Conglomerate sent to acquire it.

Illmar moved as fast as he could out of the cockpit. Entering the cargo bay, he saw the Grevax was no longer devouring Ligee. Remains were left, but it was clear Ligee's spirit had already departed the mortal realm. Illmar reached down and grabbed the restraints, then tossed them to the Grevax. It caught them with a puzzled expression, staring intently at Illmar.

"Put those on," Illmar said, placing Ligee's wristchron on its wrist. "I won't be activating them. Make sure they don't fall off until I give a signal to act. There are visitors outside we must deal with." He crossed the cargo bay to lockers along the starboard side. Opening the only unsecured one, he found his gear inside. He secured his tactical belt around his waist and pulled the Thorsen hand cannon from its holster. Bringing it to eye level, he inspected it and found it still in operative condition. He left his pulse rifle in the locker—no time to set up correctly to use it, and it wasn't as valuable as the hand cannon.

Turning from the locker, he saw the Grevax already waiting at the top of the ramp extended down from the cargo bay into the dockyard. He put Lucy back in its holster and joined the Grevax.

"Ready for some fun?" Illmar asked.

"We are..." it replied. "We don't care for those that await us outside." Illmar cast a questioning glance at the Grevax. This wasn't like the one-word syllable responses it had given before. It was as if after consuming Ligee, it had acquired some of his intellect and referred to itself as "we." He knew Grevax kind operated like a hivemind, but to ingest biological data and acquire it while maintaining that reference... No wonder the Conglomerate was here to capture this creature.

Illmar and the Grevax walked down the exit ramp. The Conglomerate's ship was ahead, but the other three landing pads were devoid of spacecraft save for a lone cargo hover idle to the left of Ligee's ship. Two biotechs were spaced out on either side behind green cargo containers with laser pistols drawn. The other two were nowhere to be seen, but the human hybrid agent stood before them. He hadn't drawn his own pulse pistol secured at his side. Illmar motioned the Grevax forward as if delivering the goods.

"You are not Ligee," the agent said. He placed his hand on the pulse pistol and squinted at Illmar. His face was rather plebian—no oversized or unique features, sporting a shaved head.

Illmar moved closer to the Grevax and placed his right hand on its back. "I am definitely not Ligee. He is in pieces aboard the ship and inside this creature you seek." Without hesitation, he vaulted onto the Grevax. He'd never had formal equestrian training, but it felt like an appropriate response to the stiffs surrounding him.

"We approve," the Grevax said as it bounded toward the nearest biotech. Before the tech could react, the Grevax picked her up and bit into her neck. She was petite and the Grevax tossed her aside like a ragdoll. Illmar fired at the other technician twelve meters from them. The tech looked down at his chest where there was now a fist-sized hole. He slumped against the cargo container, leaving a trail of blood as he fell.

The agent fired two shots from his pulse pistol at the Grevax and Illmar. The first hit the Grevax in its right shoulder, the other hit Illmar in his right arm. Still on the grevax's back, he switched Lucy to his left hand and aimed at the agent. Leaning forward, he fired, barely missing, and the Grevax let out a deep howl. It then charged toward the agent. The agent did the same, holstering his pistol and flexing its second set of arms.

They hit each other straight on, locking arms. Illmar fell off the Grevax, landing hard on his damaged arm. He gripped Lucy, not wanting to drop the weapon but finding it hard to concentrate enough to fire another round. The agent's barbed arms dug into the Grevax with barbs and talons, retracting them several times, tearing into the Grevax. This didn't seem to phase the Grevax—it bit into the side of the agent's face, pulled away its mouth and spat out a piece of the agent's cheek.

The alien arms arched back and with one quick motion, the barbs were now in the side of the Grevax's neck. Illmar could see the Grevax was starting to lose the fight. He was drifting in and out of consciousness with the amount of blood he'd been losing. Now that the agent was standing still, continuing to press its barbs into the Grevax, he aimed

Lucy center mass. Taking a deep breath, he pulled the trigger. The round hit the agent in its chest, sending it backward from the Grevax.

The Grevax moved toward the agent and pummeled him with each of its fists. The agent had a wound in his chest, but it wasn't as deep as the tech's had been, and it continued to return blows to the Grevax with its enhanced arms.

With one eye swollen and the other hanging from its socket, the Grevax pounced on the agent and opened its mouth wide. The agent brought his arms back to try another attack, but Illmar had steadied himself on one of the cargo containers and fired round after round, decimating the arms into bloody pulp. When he paused, the Grevax dug into the neck of the agent with its maw, and the agent ceased to struggle.

The Grevax pushed the agent away and spat out the massive chunk it had bitten off. Illmar sat on the ground beside the cargo container, holstered Lucy, and clutched his right arm with his left hand, trying to stop the flow of blood.

The Conglomerate ship steadily rose from its landing pad. The two techs who had been nowhere around after they'd exited Ligee's ship must have been on board and noticed the battle was over. They didn't want any part of what Illmar and the Grevax would do to them if they decided to interfere.

Illmar had stopped the blood flow on his right arm. He noticed in the skyline two ships traveling in their direction. Dusk had just set and the clouds were full. It looked like a storm could start any time, and he still didn't know what planet they were on. He'd never been to this dockyard or seen the logo stamped on the cargo containers—a fish with weird-looking serrated fins, painted with stencils, not prefabricated print.

As the ships approached, he'd never seen a design like them. The hulls weren't made of the usual metal filaments but looked like obsidian whale skin. Where chainglass would normally adorn the cockpit if there were viewports, there was one continuous membrane. Lights along the craft had an unusual purple glow, similar to the Grevax's eyes.

Both ships abruptly stopped when over the landing pads, and as they lowered, tentacles sprouted from the underside, extending downward.

"Fucking weird." The Grevax was now standing next to Illmar and had assisted him with a bandage. "What kind of landing gear is that?"

"It is more optimal than the ships your kind make," the Grevax said. "We aren't wasteful as humans and everything the universe has spawned is our inspiration."

There wasn't the clang of metal that landing gear made as the two ships rested on their landing pads. Instead, there was a loud suction sound, and at the same time, a ripple on the port side of the ships as creatures exited. They had similar skin to the Grevax he'd fought with but were smaller, closer to Earth predator felines, except with extra appendages terminating in hooks. Illmar assumed they were great for collecting the precious biomatter that Grevax kind voraciously consumed to try and perfect themselves. He just hoped he wasn't the next meal and that how he'd helped the Grevax would be taken into consideration.

After eight of the feline monstrosities circled Illmar and the Grevax, a lone human figure emerged from the same undulating portal on the ship to his right. He wore a grey shipsuit with no designs anywhere. Long black hair, clean-shaven. His eyes gave him away—they matched the Grevax's, and Illmar couldn't tell if this supposed human had a soul as he felt emptiness looking into them.

"Illmar..." the human said, extending a hand. Illmar shook it, trying not to be repulsed by the strong smell of sulfur. It was more pungent than the scent the Grevax had given off when he'd ridden it into battle. "You have no idea how you have helped us. We were looking for this proto-grevax you encountered on Jilarska. We thought we had her tracked down there and were about to intercept, but then we saw her signal disappear and end up on Viria."

"Proto-grevax?" Illmar was starting to have problems standing again. He wasn't sure how damaged his right arm was, but he could no longer feel the pain from earlier.

"Yes," the human said. "We were made in a lab with intent on us becoming a weapon to be wielded. Instead, the Biosphere Conglomerate leader at the time, some 1500 years ago, gave our earliest forms too much agency. We escaped and took care of our own destiny."

"So what is your purpose then?" Illmar hoped it didn't include them using his biomatter for their destiny.

"First to eradicate our creators," the human said with a determined look. "Don't worry Illmar, we may have motives that would be hard for you to understand, but we do help those who help us with the Conglomerate." He turned from Illmar and motioned for him to follow. "We will fix you up and bring you back to your ship. If you're looking for work, we can supply you with that and more funds than those backward bounty offices can offer."

Even though the original Grevax was just as battered as Illmar, she picked him up with her arms and carried him to the Grevaxian's human ship. She stepped into the portal and the sensation was nothing like he'd felt before. It was like if hundreds of octopi had caressed him with their suckers. He hated to admit it, but it was kind of soothing compared to what he'd just gone through. She placed Illmar onto a nearby table made of the same material as the ship—it looked as if it had been grown out of the ship's floor instead of placed there.

A floating sphere hovered over Illmar as he lay on the table. Tentacles sprouted from the obsidian sphere and covered him from head to toe.

"Try to relax," the human said over a speaker. There was no one in the room with him. He hadn't noticed the Grevax or the human hybrid leave. The feline creatures were also nowhere to be seen. The only light came from an eerie purplish glow from optical lenses that aligned the room. They were more like eyes than lights or monitoring devices. "You will be restored soon. Hopefully our process won't alter you. It is hard to judge how our tech affects those who come into contact with it."

Illmar thought he heard an underlying current of humor when the Grevaxian human had spoken. It didn't matter though—he was just happy he'd survived the ordeal. And whatever those tentacles were injecting him with were some of the smoothest painkillers he'd ever experienced...

✦ · · · ✦

Illmar woke abruptly as his Grevax friend lowered him into a chair. He'd been dreaming about the last mug of ale at Torafa's Grill before he'd left for Jilarska. He was startled to find she'd set him in the cockpit of his cruiser. It was just as he'd left it before meeting Ligee and the Grevax. He noticed he was wearing a similar flightsuit to what the human hybrid had worn. At least the clothing wasn't made of the same whale-like skin of the shuttle or adorned with tentacles.

"I must leave you now," the Grevax said. She was leaning over Illmar, having to bend her knees to move about the cockpit. As she left his ship, he noticed on one of his systems panels there were coordinates that had been entered. On closer examination, there were also details about a target that needed to be eliminated and the pay.

Illmar let out a low whistle. It had been a long time since he'd seen a bounty like that. They'd already deposited half into one of his accounts—more than enough for him to find a hotel near his new destination and enjoy the local bars' finest offerings. He plugged the coordinates into his ship's network and gave the commands to make the jump.

He sat back in the captain's chair and sighed with great relief. There was nothing like traveling the cosmos and partaking in its splendor. If his newfound friends continued to pay him like that, it wouldn't be long before he could open up his own pub and retire.

Anom Never Sleeps

Harper Kurosawa crept through the debris field at the edge of what used to be Finrais. Dusk was settling in, and normally she'd welcome the darkness—small and quiet as she was, night had always been her ally. But Anom's drones didn't hunt by sight alone, and his combat mechs patrolled the surface with sensors that made traditional cover worthless.

The dark green field suit was supposed to help with that. Heat masking material, state of the art according to the quartermaster. Harper had watched it fail too many times to trust it. Operatives staying perfectly still, doing everything right, and still getting incinerated. Anom was always upgrading, always adapting. Had to be tracking more than heat signatures and bio readings.

Anom didn't leave survivors. His love for Earth and the animals there far surpassed whatever he felt for the ones he called "feral apes".

A single drone was fast approaching her location—right there on her scanner. Had she been seen or was it just passing by? No way to know. Harper powered down her scanner and Polaris sidearm. Only enough charge on the sidearm for a few shots or for one large EM blast that could disable multiple drones or robots. If she turned it off she might not be able to start it up again but she had to take the chance. She did have her father's katana strapped to her back but she saved that as a last resort and it was usually not that effective against beings made of steel or plascrete.

Too far away from any known outpost to try and make a run for it if she'd been spotted. And no help coming—Asher hadn't sent the signal that he'd finished delivering High Command's message and was on his way.

The mound of debris in front of her was full of derelict electronic devices and parts of a nearby building that had been demolished. Harper remained low and close to the ground. The drone scanning on the other side of her location—she could hear it now. Single drones weren't usually something to be feared unless they were a forward scout for a larger patrol. Even though Anom had begun to terraform Earth near locations around his monoliths, he hadn't completed his primary goal and was still foraging for materials like the leftover human factions had been for the last millennium.

The sounds of the drone's scanning were coming dreadfully close. Harper didn't want to take any chances. Had to take it down and leave the area as soon as possible.

At least it was a scout. Anom kept his long-range weapons near the monoliths—for large scale assaults or defense. The scouts were built to find targets, not kill them efficiently. Small mercy. He'd been designed as a terraforming platform to save Earth, and he'd excelled at that. Forests were growing again, faster than anything the Orsen Republic had managed.

Humanity had built Anom to repair what they'd destroyed. Instead, the Haeolt Collective and the other corporations had fled to their colonies, leaving Earth with a digital god that hated its creators.

The sounds of the drone's scanning and suspensor motor stopped. Harper froze, listening.

She tried powering up her Polaris sidearm. The scout drone veered hard around the corner and when it spotted her it started scanning again. It ascended at an alarming rate and a compartment opened underneath. The sound of whirring motors emanated and a small cannon sprang out from the compartment.

Without hesitation, Harper moved from the debris pile as fast as she could to the nearby ruins of a building. The roof was gone and so were several sections of the walls. The drone followed in pursuit and started lobbing napalm rounds ahead of where she was running to. When they hit the ground they ignited, catching anything flammable on fire—worse than any flame thrower she'd faced.

Harper made it to a section of wall that looked sturdy. Part of the second floor was still above her when she rounded the corner, and there were enough gaps in the broken masonry that she could climb. She pulled herself up and reached what remained of the second story. The floor was holding for the moment and she kept her right hand on the wall just in case it collapsed. The last thing she needed was to fall and break a leg, unable to move away from the raging inferno below.

The drone kept launching incendiary rounds that had to be made of gel clusters filled with napalm. When they hit the ground, even if there wasn't any foliage or flammable waste, it ignited and burned for a couple of minutes. At least it didn't seem to be that accurate but that could mean that a patrol was nearby because this wasn't the typical armament for a lone scouting drone.

When the drone hovered around the corner, Harper saw her chance. She drew the katana from its saya with her right hand and brought it around to her front, raising it high with both hands, blade pointed toward the drone's exposed undercarriage. She leapt and thrust upward, driving the tip of the katana into the compartment where the napalm cannon extended. The blade punched through and caught on something solid inside. She held onto her family heirloom as tight as possible, her full weight now hanging from the sword.

The drone lurched violently sideways, trying to dislodge both weapon and attacker. It slammed into the wall and Harper felt the impact shudder through the blade into her arms. The collision cracked the drone's casing wide open. She wrenched the katana free as they fell, managing to maintain her grip as napalm gel canisters spilled out and hit the ground around them.

She didn't lose any time as she sprinted away, jumping over patches of the ground that were still on fire and trying best to pick out a path where she wouldn't end up getting burnt. Her right pant leg caught on fire and as she was running to a nearby forest, she unbuttoned the top of her field suit, stopped to peel it off, then grabbed the katana in its saya before the saya caught on fire. The holster to the Polaris sidearm had caught fire since it was close to her leg but it wasn't as precious to her as the sword so she left it behind. The sidearm probably wouldn't function again anyway and she didn't have any fuel cells left.

Holding the katana in her left hand, she continued moving towards her target destination. The suit had protected her from her legs getting burnt and so did her field gloves but she had to leave them behind as they caught on fire when she touched the pantlegs.

In her line of work she'd been in worse situations than running in her boots, sports bra, and underwear. Anything was better than being burnt alive and having to smell your own burnt flesh.

The forest was to the west of Finrais and it was full of maples, elms, and oaks. She wished she wasn't in a hurry to get there, wasn't trying to continue traveling away from where she'd been spotted. After having lived underground in subterranean caverns and outposts for over twenty five years, it was always nice to find patches of greenery and spend as much time as she could admiring it.

Before Anom landed over one hundred years ago, trees had been a rarity. Now forests grew everywhere—but they belonged to Anom, and forests of this size were usually too close to the areas he'd claimed.

The sound of mechanized movement came from the direction she was moving in. Close to the edge of the forest now, and when Harper looked over her shoulder to the east, the majority of what was left of Finrais was on fire. Instead of entering the forest, she ran parallel to its edge. The night was getting colder, with winter having just ended and the warm part of spring not yet started. She'd need to find shelter soon but without her scanner, it would be hard to find her way back to her assigned outpost if she continued in the opposite direction in territory she'd never been in before.

She picked up her speed hoping it was enough to get far away from what could be coming from the forest. There was a rock formation up ahead and she made her way towards it. She placed her hand on the closest boulder to her and pivoted behind it. The sounds of the machines approaching was growing louder. There was also the noticeable sound of gravitational motors in the cacophony and that could only be the sound of either a grav-bike or assault drones that supported the combat mechs.

The assault drones were not like the teardrop shaped scout drones that were sleek and built for travel. They were slower and appeared to be floating ponderously, that is until they found their target. Even though Harper was a soldier and well conditioned, she still wouldn't be able to outrun an assault drone.

Climbing the grey boulder she'd moved behind, and then steadying herself on the one that was resting on top of it, she leaned out to get a better view of what would probably lead to her demise. There was a group of five combat mechs approaching with a pair of assault drones escorting them. The mechs were over ten feet in height with batteries of cannons on either side. Their segmented legs moved in frightening efficiency. Swarms of beetles ran across the AI powered cockpits.

The beetles were also machines. They were usually seen throughout the forests that Anom had repopulated spraying water and other nutrients on the trees and underbrush. When they were accompanying one of Anom's death patrols they were far more insidious. If the cannons of the mechs or the flame throwers on an assault drone didn't get you, they would send out the beetles to inject their victims with a sleeping agent so the patrols would catch them. Other times Harper had witnessed them bore into her fellow soldiers leaving behind hundreds of tiny holes, puncturing vital organs in the process.

As they moved closer, she realized that they weren't coming after her. There was a lone rider on top of a grav-bike weaving in and out of the edge of the forest, knocking over tree branches with a pair of pulse cannons that were on the side of the grav-bike.

At first this could be her chance to escape. They would continue their focus on the grav-bike, hot in pursuit of a better target but then she noticed it was Asher. The patrol had to have found him when he was traveling to assist Harper. No idea how she would be able to change the situation that he was now facing but she'd learned one thing in all her years serving Orsen's Republic—you never leave a comrade on their own, no matter the situation.

The machines were cold and heartless, only concerned about their total domination of Humankind. Even though the remaining members of humanity on Earth were in survival mode, they had to differentiate themselves from those who were hunting them, otherwise they wouldn't be any different. Harper believed this in her very core and as she stood on the boulder in her underwear and combat boots, she readied her katana, looking for her chance to enter the fray when they moved past her.

Right before Asher approached the rock formation, he weaved into the edge of the forest, taking aim at more trees. This time he managed to knock over a cluster of eight or so trunks and they tumbled in the direction of the machines. The mechs paused for a moment taking defensive positions while opening fire at the grav-bike and the lumber that was tumbling their way.

He swung out wide from the rock formation and Harper's heart sunk. If he was changing course and then picking up speed, she would definitely be left behind and there was a chance that they would still intercept him. Instead of continuing on that path, he fired more rounds from the dual pulse cannons, scoring direct hits on the assault drones closest to him. He turned the bike again and doubled back to her position. As he moved closer to the rock formation, he slowed down and looked up in the general direction where she was located.

"It's a good thing they put more than one tracking device in our uniforms," Asher said as he motioned for Harper to hurry. She jumped down and crossed over to the grav-bike as fast as her already tired legs would carry her. "I found the other part of your uniform, glad the rest of you was with your boots."

Harper climbed on the back of the grav-bike and secured herself by reaching around Asher. She checked to make sure she still had her father's katana. Even though it would be too late to go back and retrieve it if left behind, what she had left to remember her father by was always comforting. She didn't have much left of her parents, only the katana and her memories of them.

As if Asher had been playing with the combat patrol with his previous driving routine, he pushed the limits of what the grav-bike could do, trying his best to lose his hunters. Off in the distance the terrain climbed and he made his way for the foothills.

Harper was glad that Asher had arrived when he did but at the same time there had to be something else going on. He wasn't supposed to be rendezvousing with her at least for another day, despite that he'd missed the check-in call she'd sent out a day before. She'd been worried that he'd been delayed and she would have to find a way to stay hidden from further patrols with no supplies. She was skilled and had done so before but only by the skin of her teeth.

She peered behind her the best she could. No sign of the combat patrols or scouting drones following them. She breathed a sigh of relief and relaxed her grip on him. "I think we have lost them."

"Indeed we have," Asher said as he slowed down after confirming on the sensor portion of the grav-bike HUD. It was the standard grav-bike that the Orsen Republic issued, big enough to fit two soldiers and their gear. The twin-linked pulse cannons were a welcome addition that had been added in the last ten years as their weapon technology kept improving. The electronic camouflage that covered the main part of the bike had already switched over from the patterns that matched the forests to a more subdued color pattern that blended in better with the surrounding foothills.

When they came upon a ravine deep enough to conceal the bike from any long distance viewing devices, Asher maneuvered down into it and the bike slowed to a hovering rest position.

Besides the fact that she was hardly wearing any clothes, Harper resisted embracing Asher. There had been more than one occasion where they'd been close to crossing the boundaries that most soldiers kept, even when alcohol hadn't been involved. The Republic didn't necessarily frown on relationships in the ranks as it had been hard to have positive birthrates since the Last Wars and Anom's arrival on Earth.

It wouldn't bother her if she became pregnant, it would be an honor to help bolster the ranks of the Orsen Republic. She just took after her father and had too much of the warrior spirit left in her at her young age. There would be time to have children if she managed to survive.

"Here you go," Asher said with a sly grin on his face. "It isn't a bad look for you but I think you might want more clothing for our next set of orders." He tossed her a gear bag that she recognized belonged to her. There wasn't another heat masking suit inside, but there was a set of fatigues she used when working on base.

Dawn was fast approaching and on top of exhaustion, she was beginning to feel famished. She'd down a few tubes of concentrates that was sure to be in Asher's saddlebags and was hoping he had something with caffeine in it as well. She found a cylinder of cold-brew that was somewhat adequate but not quite and gulped it down as fast as she could.

"So what are our next orders?" Harper asked as she wiped off some cold-brew that had spilled on her chin. It wasn't the same as the French Press coffee Asher was famous for in their unit, but it would suffice.

"We are to take down a new operation that we think was started by a segregated copy of Anom's mind," he said as he himself ate some of the concentrate. "Or we at least hope is a copy of Anom's mind. We don't want the main Anom to get any more ideas in how to torture or use us."

He had a grim look on his face and Harper knew that it had to be something only Anom was capable of. Asher was a battle hardened soldier and had been in plenty of conflicts, witnessing plenty of Anom's handiwork.

"It's too hard to put into words. I will have to take you to a safe distance where you can see it yourself."

The ride to the perimeter had been uneventful. No more signs of patrols and the day had been warmer than the previous one. The light breeze was enjoyable but that didn't last long as they arrived at the edge of the new operation that the robots had been working on. The hastily built construction site was inside another forest, this one being less dense than the one Harper had been to the night before.

Asher powered down the grav-bike, hiding it behind a pile of debris that was close to the edge of the forest. The forest was comprised mainly of eastern white pines, trees that had been here from before the Last Wars and even though Anom hated them, he was good at preserving nature.

Harper followed Asher as he made his way to the edge of the forest. He paused when he was next to a rather large pine and pointed inside the forest.

Not more than fifty feet from their location, up on branches that were a few stories high—shapes that looked almost human, but twisted and incomplete. She pulled up the monocular that Asher had handed her and adjusted the focus.

They were attached to the branches at the wrists, arms spread wide like they were hanging laundry. Their skin was stretched taut, translucent in places where the afternoon light filtered through. It looked like all of their bones had been ripped out of them, leaving only the outer layer of skin sagging in the middle. Someone had purposefully done this and was drying out their outer layer of skin like leather, like they were preparing to wear it later as a garment.

The damned machine beetles were crawling all over them and must be spraying them with some kind of filament to strengthen them. Where the beetles had already worked, the skin started to shine when sunlight broke free from the top of the canopy of the forest, taking on an almost crystalline quality.

Harper's hand tightened on the monocular. Her throat constricted. Not a scream of fright trying to escape, but one of anguish. There was no telling what they had to go through before ending up as sick and twisted decorations. How long had they been alive during the process? It was as if they were no more than abstract art for a deranged individual who cherished the grotesque.

She counted seven of them. Seven people who'd woken up that morning not knowing this would be their fate.

She looked at Asher and he glanced at her. Without saying anything, she knew that he was thinking the same thing and why it had been hard to talk about what they were facing in length. He touched her wristchron and closed his eyes. The forefinger and middle finger that he touched the wristchron with was coated in a protective layer that could switch to a conductive one to interface with augs and computer terminals.

He must be using a thought impulse to create a message for a direct download to her wristchron. When he finished, he let go of her wristchron and motioned for the monocle.

Harper looked down at her wristchron:

We don't think this is Anom's doing. Has to be a copy because there aren't any signals being broadcasted or patrols that have connected with this location. Follow my lead, we are to take down this site by all means necessary.

They didn't have their service rifles but Asher had packed backup Polaris sidearms along with energy cells on the grav-bike. In the field suit that he wore, he had several explosive compounds along with detonators.

Harper had also managed to grab three plasma grenades. They were best used as a last resort but she would be more than happy to use them—even at the cost of her life—if they stopped the crime against humanity that was before them.

He crossed over to another pine, careful to avoid arousing any suspicion from robots that were working at this site. For the moment none of them were seen and dusk was setting in.

She didn't dare to look upward. Bad enough during the daylight and she was sure to have nightmares from what she'd seen. She didn't need to give that part of her subconscious any more fuel.

Harper followed Asher closely and saw that there was ground that had been dug up directly below from where the boneless humans were hanging. The sides of the hole were reinforced and it was apparent that the reason that they didn't see any robots after they arrived was due to them probably working underground.

After rounding a few more trees and getting closer to the entrance, she paused when something emerged from the freshly dug hole in the ground. At first it was only the head of an android and it appeared to be scanning its surroundings. Anom hated humanity but he still used their form in some of his machines because it was more agile and could carry items in tunnels or other compartments where smaller drones weren't as optimal.

The android had not seen Harper or Asher. If it had, it wasn't betraying that it knew of their location. It continued moving out of the hole and then reached down inside. It dragged a female human body that was dressed in similar uniform to Asher. At the distance they were at and with the dim lighting, Harper couldn't see the face of the female soldier. Probably best that she couldn't because if she'd recognized the face it would have been hard for her to not give away their position.

"Why are you doing this?" the female soldier said in a hoarse voice. The android said nothing in return and it hoisted the soldier over its mechanical shoulder. It was the standard design that Anom used, approximately six foot tall, recycled metal was used to fashion it, and it had sleek contour panels covering where skin would be on a human. Its eyes were made out of optical cable, close to a human's eye but very much in an odd uncanny way.

As it moved towards the closest tree to where the other boneless humans were hanging from it dropped the female soldier to the ground. She looked up at it first with disgust and hatred but when it raised its hand upwards as if it was going to strike her there was a look that was pleading for mercy. Its hand fell and broke her neck with an efficient twist.

A circular saw popped out from a compartment located on the bottom of its forearm and then it sawed open the wrists and ankles of the woman.

Harper grimaced and bit down on her bottom lip. She didn't want to see what was probably going to happen next. She'd been paying too much attention to the android and hadn't noticed that Asher had inched his way close to where the hole in the ground was. He was dirty from moving along the ground and there was pine straw in his hair. He sprang into action as the android reached down and began breaking the bones in the woman's arms and legs.

Harper moved to assist him. She pulled up her sidearm and aimed it at the android. Right before Asher was on the machine, she fired three low powered shots in its direction. The first one missed and the android turned, dropping the arm of the woman it had been holding. The other two connected, one scoring a direct hit at the base of the android's head. These weren't designed for battle and Asher caught it as it fell to the ground, rendered inoperable from Harper's attack.

There was a slight chance that the android had sent warning signals back to wherever it was receiving commands from but Harper hoped they'd acted fast enough. The machines here weren't sending signals back and forth to Anom's other installations so it was possible that for some reason, the group here was experiencing some kind of technical difficulties.

Asher lowered the android to the ground and slowly crossed over to the entrance of the underground tunnel. He paused for a moment, carefully checking the entrance below, and Harper joined him.

There was no lighting and she pulled out a pair of night vision goggles that was part of her standard kit. As she donned hers, Asher did the same and they both started going down the tunnel. She pulled out her sidearm, and held it in the ready position.

The tunnel on either side had been reinforced with plascrete beams and the soil was a mixture of glacial till. It widened as it progressed and there was a segment autolayer—a bulky ground vehicle with large wheels, drill on the front, and beam inserter on the back—not too far from the entrance. When Harper switched from thermal imaging on her goggles to near-infrared, she could see streaks of blood stains where previous victims had been dragged across the tunnel. The stains were everywhere. Walls, floor, even smeared across the low ceiling where someone must have tried to brace themselves.

They walked slowly, side by side, coordinating their movement, checking for any new entrances into the main tunnel that they were now traveling through. Not more than fifty feet ahead of their position, Harper paused when she became aware that the tunnel widened drastically outward.

Her pace and Asher's slowed to a crawl as they approached the area in the tunnel where it widened. A faint hum reverberated in the distance and an odd greenish glow illuminated the opening that she was standing next to. The tunnel emptied into an underground cavern.

The air changed. It smelled of copper and chemicals—antiseptic mixed with blood, like a field hospital and slaughterhouse combined. Something else too—ozone and heated metal, the smell of active machinery.

In the dim light it was hard for Harper to know the cavern's full dimensions but in the center was a chambered set of rooms. The sides of the chambers took on the eerie glow and there were a total of nine of them. Each one had chainglass bay windows that extended into the cavern.

She lowered her night vision goggles.

In all of the windows there was one of the stretched out human beings. At this distance it was hard to make out their facial features but their stretched out skin was suspended by a set of racks made out of a combination of plascrete and chainglass. The racks looked almost medical, like something from a hospital but corrupted for a twisted use.

Harper's breathing came shallow. She had to force herself to look, to understand what she was seeing.

A pair of androids was next to each rack and as if it was a cue to continue work when Harper and Asher arrived, they began inserting mechanical limbs into the incisions on the humans' wrists. The sound of servos whirring and metal sliding into flesh echoed through the cavern. One of the bodies twitched.

Harper wanted to go in guns blazing, destroying this monstrosity, hating to even imagine what the finished product would look like. Whoever was behind this would have to pay for the abomination she was witnessing. She raised her sidearm in her right hand and traced a finger over one of the plasma grenades on her belt.

In the center chamber a bald male human approached the chainglass bay window. On his head there were square precious metal nodes arranged in a grid pattern—neural interface nodes. Harper pivoted slightly, aiming her sidearm at the man. Three android assistants flanked him on either side. His eyes widened as he noticed Harper and Asher. It was as if he was delighted by their arrival, like they were expected guests. She was determined not to end up like the other victims in the cavern.

Asher motioned for her to cover him and he dashed to the side of the first chamber on the left of the center one. He slapped an explosive on the side of it and then moved over to the main chamber. He repeated the process and picked up his pace as he continued down the row of chambers.

The sound of a gate retracting echoed throughout the cavern and androids popped out of a corridor from the left side. They carried pulse rifles. This confused Harper as this was not standard issue weaponry that she'd seen on any of Anom's creations. He did use long range ammunition but it was in his fleets and not in android patrols. He preferred using drones and mechs for combat instead of human form machines.

The man could be from one of the groups that left Earth—the ones who'd built the colony ships and abandoned the planet. They were responsible for the platform that brought Anom in the first place. The Haeolt Collective and their corporate partners.

Harper tightened her grip on her sidearm and rolled to the side of the cavern, firing one high powered round towards the androids that approached Asher from the corridor. The blast deactivated all but one of them. It took aim at Asher and before Harper could turn towards the android, it scored a direct hit in the center of Asher's back. He fell to the cavern floor, dropping the last charge that he had and the detonator. There was a gash in his back and blood seeped out from the wound, over the edge of his torn fieldsuit.

Changing energy cells from her sidearm, Harper fired several low powered energy rounds. All of them missed but she closed in on the last standing android as it leveled its rifle at her. She slid towards it as it fired a round, and regaining focus, she scored a direct hit underneath its chin, shattering the metal and wiring that connected the head to its body. She stood and pushed the android over.

"Are you looking for this," a nasally voice said. Harper turned in its direction. It was the man that had been in the center chamber. He had Asher's detonator in his left hand and a pulse pistol in the other. His android assistants were trying to undo the explosives that Asher had planted. "Why would you want to destroy such beautiful creations?"

"So you are the madman behind this?" Harper holstered her sidearm and pulled out a plasma grenade, pressing it twice with her palm. If any of the man's androids attacked her and she dropped it, the charge was large enough to create a cave in. The other explosives were certain to be ignited with the blast wave and the macabre creations in front of her would no longer exist.

"Madman?" The man looked genuinely puzzled. He was frail and thin as if he hadn't eaten in weeks, his work more important than sustenance. "No I am Thurfield, one of the

Haeolt Collective's biotechs. I gather from my reconnaissance that you think Anom was a mistake. He wasn't a mistake, just needs an update."

"You call this an update?" Harper moved closer to Thurfield. The androids so far had only been able to remove one of the explosives. They hadn't dismantled it yet and she was close enough now that if they managed and then retrieved the others, she would be able to use the plasma grenade instead to carry out her and Asher's mission.

With her other hand, she withdrew her katana from its saya. If she wasn't pressed to use the plasma grenade, this piece of shit deserved retribution from her father's blade.

"Anom exterminates humans because he sees us as a threat to the ecosystem," Thurfield continued, as if lecturing a student. "But what if we became part of the ecosystem? What if we were the trees?" He gestured to the chambers with genuine pride. "Living support structures for his forests. Sustainable. Elegant."

Behind Thurfield, Asher slowly rose to his knees. Harper resheathed her katana as she had an idea what Asher was about to do. The bald man gave her a questioning look before it turned into dreadful delight. He must have thought that she was going to give up, knowing her fate would soon be like the other soldiers.

Before the biotech noticed Asher, he hit the man in his legs and grabbed the detonator. "Run."

Harper didn't give it a second thought and turned away from them, crossing the chamber, moving as fast as she could towards the tunnel.

"How could you, so much potential wasted," Thurfield said, his voice rising in genuine anguish.

The explosion was deafening. The shockwave hit Harper's back like a fist and she stumbled but kept moving. She bit back tears as the tunnel collapsed behind her, dust filling her mouth and nose as she scrambled in the dark toward the entrance. The sound of the chambers imploding echoed up through the tunnel—metal shrieking, glass shattering, and underneath it all, mercifully, the destruction of those twisted experiments.

All she could think about was Asher. She didn't care about the wasted potential that this man from the collective perceived or the robots that might greet her as she surfaced.

The wasted potential was Asher. They'd served together fighting what seemed to be a hopeless cause. Anom never slept, constantly hunting them and now there were other groups potentially hunting them too, and human in origin. The people who'd left Earth behind were coming back with their own twisted solutions.

As Harper neared the entrance of the tunnel, she slowed down and peered outside. Still dark and there was no apparent movement of animal or machine. Her wristchron would guide her to where their grav-bike was located. Pressing the plasma grenade three times which would trigger a 10 second delay, she dropped it into the tunnel.

Even if he hadn't detonated the explosives, Asher had appeared to be close to death and she couldn't let Thurfield or any of his creations escape. She wouldn't have time to retrieve the rest of her fellow humans that were disgracefully hung in the canopy of the forest but she could give them a funeral pyre with her remaining plasma grenades.

Harper pulled the other two grenades from her belt and armed them both, then moved through the forest to where the stretched bodies hung from the branches. She couldn't look at their faces, just threw the grenades at the base of the trees and ran.

The forest erupted behind her. The plasma grenades ignited the pines and the flames spread fast through the dry needles. The smell was almost unbearable—burning wood and something worse that Harper tried not to think about. The ground beneath still reverberated with tremors of underground tunnels and buildings collapsing.

Harper mounted the grav-bike. Her hands were shaking as she powered it up. The bike hummed to life and she drove off in the direction of the nearest outpost.

She hadn't beheaded Thurfield like she'd wanted. That bothered her more than it should. But there would be other time for that in the future if the Haeolt Collective ever dared to show itself on Earth again.

The bike picked up speed and Harper let herself cry—not much, just enough to clear the dust from her eyes and honor what Asher had done. When she got back to base, she'd file her report, tell them about Thurfield and the Collective, tell them that humanity's enemies weren't just on Earth anymore.

For now, she had her memories of Asher. His wonderful French Press coffee. The way he'd doubled back for her without hesitation. The last word he'd said.

Run.

She would. For both of them. And then, she would return when the moment was right for retribution with her father's blade.

The Grevax Vendetta

Exen Rual huddled close to Iona Jayden inside the drop pod. Unlike standard planetary insertion vehicles, this was a stealth variant designed to integrate with molecular awareness. The cramped interior forced them into a hunched posture over the central control panel. Trajectory data scrolled past—velocity, altitude, seconds to phase shift.

With his awareness active, Exen had to concentrate to avoid losing himself in the interaction between air molecules and his skin, the pod's walls, the microscopic dance of matter that most beings never perceived. He and Iona were initiate Shapers of the Order of Infinity, and molecular awareness was both gift and distraction.

"We're close to transition altitude," Iona said.

Exen leaned back, hands pressing against the pod's interior. Iona mirrored him. They stood simultaneously, eyes closing in trained synchronization. The chrominthium core activated inside his skull—a psychenetic accelerator forged from interdimensional alloy. It reached beyond the standard four dimensions, granting Shapers the power to manipulate matter through their awareness.

The walls shifted to translucence. Exen opened his eyes. Time to phase.

He projected his awareness onto both the pod and his own body, then translated his physical form outside the vehicle in a single instant. One mistake meant death. Or worse—a rift that would consume the planet if no experienced Shaper intervened.

Wind slammed into him, forcing a squint. Iona materialized beside him, her phase shift flawless. They fell like skydivers as the pod fragmented above them, pieces that would burn to nothing before reaching the surface.

Iona spread her arms and linked with him. She pointed at her wristchron. Impact approached. Exen prepared for another phase shift while Iona readied herself to displace their inertia upon rematerialization.

The ground rushed up. He phased an instant before fatal impact. During training, they'd performed these maneuvers countless times, but never with actual death as the alternative. He kept his face neutral despite the concern grinding through his thoughts.

They blinked between dimensions and reappeared. Exen grunted as his feet struck ground harder than expected. Pain shot through his legs. His mind raced—damage assessment, structural integrity—but after a moment, he looked down. Nothing was broken.

Iona leaned close, lips near his ear. "Did that on purpose. Good to keep your guard up." She winked and pivoted into a crouch. Exen followed, scanning their surroundings for witnesses.

This training exercise formed part of their final exam. Complete the objectives on Nullwind undetected, reach the rendezvous on schedule, and upon returning to Order headquarters they'd graduate from initiates to full Shapers. Exen had family who would celebrate this accomplishment. For Iona, the Order was all she had.

Before becoming an initiate, Iona had worked as a planetologist. She'd already synced her wristchron to their first objective's general direction. They needed to apprehend a Shaper from their Order who was posing as an assassin—somewhere in one of the cities, blending with locals, positioning for a mock assassination attempt.

Exen checked his meld-armor's integrity. Black with blue marbling, the lightweight suit bent light molecules and provided protection from projectiles or energy weapons their awareness couldn't alter. Chrominthium enhanced fiber made the armor easier to manipulate, along with their standard meld-daggers and grav-discs. The small satchel remained secured on his back. He signaled Iona.

They advanced into the nearby forest adjacent to Vilnestra.

While preparing for their mission, Iona had suggested starting in Vilnestra. The city was governed by affluent interstellar tradesmen who serviced the Thorsen Empire and its planetary holdings. Council members experienced frequent "accidents" during public disputes. Recently, one such dispute had become common gossip in starport bars, with bets already placed on which council member would suffer the next unfortunate incident.

Inside the forest, they restructured their meld-armor from protective coating to thin wetsuit composition. From their satchels they pulled clothing to blend with Vilnestra's inhabitants.

They emerged from the forest onto a transit platform where locals waited for the next transport into the city. Exen adjusted his ill-fitting shirt while Iona checked their false credentials one last time. When they stepped off in Vilnestra's lower district, they were just two more young travelers disappearing into the evening crowds.

+ · · · +

Leonard stood over his victim, admiring his work. Time was short, but he had minutes to spare watching blood spread across the frigate's deck. Normally he worked with precision—most missions required eliminations that went unnoticed. This mission demanded the entire crew's death, then a delayed charge to arouse suspicion while he operated planetside.

He crouched lower, studying the spreading pattern. Each mission taught him something new about human physiology, about the precise timing between vascular damage and cardiac arrest.

To external observation, Leonard appeared human. Close inspection, especially by a medical professional, would reveal his Grevax nature. Minuscule olfactory neutralizers implanted throughout his pores masked his scent. Despite the Grevax's skill at creating subspecies—so varied they'd lost track of which form was original—they'd never bred out their odor.

Leonard missed the sulfur smell of his kind. Even the slithoids he'd brought carried the same neutralizers. On this operation he'd brought five—hybrid forms crossing scorpion and spider with chameleon camouflage. He released pheromones to issue complex commands, most importantly which chemical compounds they used on targets. All Grevax seekers deployed slithoids on clandestine operations beyond their worlds.

After the blood finished spreading, Leonard moved toward the communications room at the frigate's rear. The last living crew member lay unconscious from slithoid venom—Petty Officer 2nd Class Chelsinal Nielmi. Leonard had worked alongside her until beginning his work. She hadn't seemed suspicious of his replacement of Serviceman Derric Fensworth.

He'd already commanded the slithoids via pheromone to bind her wrists and ankles with strands. After finishing, they'd inject a stimulant with their mandibles. Their mandibles delivered stimulants or antidotes while the stinger manufactured poison or corrosive fluid. No race matched the Grevaax at genetic engineering.

Entering the communications room, Leonard surveyed the layout, checking for interruption possibilities. Communication panels lined one wall, fold-out desks with equipment lined the opposite. Two crew members slumped in the corner, dead from earlier venom injections.

Chelsinal woke in the chair, feeling strands constrict her wrists behind her back. Her feet were secured to the deck. No amount of effort moved them. Her shoulder-length hair and feminine appearance in the Thorsen Empire's dark blue uniform disguised capability Leonard recognized—she could handle someone his size.

Her mouth remained unbound but she stayed silent, staring in defiance. Leonard was impressed.

He tilted his head. The last crew members he'd personally killed—the ones the slithoids hadn't poisoned—had reeked of fear, most of them male. This one was different.

Chelsinal glanced at the corner where her crewmates displayed death's ash-gray complexion. Her eyes narrowed as she refocused on Leonard.

"You're not Derric, are you?" Her tone remained calm.

"What makes you think I'm not Derric?"

The Progenitors—the Grevax leadership who created Seekers like him—had planned Leonard's infiltration months in advance, targeting an Order of Infinity training session where initiates wouldn't have Void Sphere support. Leonard had studied every available source on Serviceman Derric Fensworth, memorizing mannerisms, speech patterns, service history. He'd become adept at infiltrating units and "replacing" individuals.

He'd enjoyed jettisoning Derric's corpse into vacuum from the space station where the frigate had docked before coming to Nullwind.

"Derric was an orphan like me. The Empire is the only place that ever showed us respect." Her voice began matching the attitude in her eyes. "You couldn't pay him enough to betray his unit...the only family he knew."

"Call me Leonard, then." The name came from his first assumed identity on his first operation. He used it when rare circumstances revealed his true nature. He moved closer as three slithoids positioned on her right shoulder while two stationed near the entrance.

"Well Leonard, just as Derric was loyal, so am I." Chelsinal spit in his face.

Leonard understood the intended insult. It was absurd. Grevax only saw bodily fluids as means to an end. He smiled, wiping the spit slowly as if cherishing it.

"Oh, simple Nielmi." He leaned over her ear, lips pursed. "Might take a few tries with different concoctions, but your kind are weak to chemical intrusions."

"Chemical intrusions? You think you're clever with your definition of torture?"

"Clever? No. Just resourceful."

✦ · · · ✦

Leonard paced across the room, hand on his right temple, perplexed by Chelsinal's resistance. He'd tried everything—removing fingernails to concoctions causing excruciating boils. Nothing worked. The harder he pushed, the fiercer her hatred burned. The terminal on the wall remained on, but hacking the interface without data from the Thorsen's system made finding the Shapers' planetary destination difficult.

Rolling her head sideways, Chelsinal opened her eyes. "I know you plan...on killing...me." Blood ran from her mouth's corner as she tried lifting her head upright. "If you let me live...send me somewhere...I can disappear...I'll give you the password."

Leonard considered. He'd planned to kill her after obtaining the password, but her non-compliance and his dwindling time suggested an alternative that might benefit the Grevax.

"I'll put you on a shuttle with a medkit." He stood directly before her chair and leaned close to her face. "I'll send you to an outpost that might give you a chance to survive. But if you don't provide the correct password, I'll ensure the shuttle first leaks enough oxygen to make breathing difficult. Then, right when you can't take the oxygen deprivation any longer, one of my slithoids will inject you with a toxin that slowly erodes your cells, resulting in a very slow, painful death as you drift through space."

Unable to keep her head upright, Chelsinal's head rolled sideways as she closed her eyes. "I will give you...what you need."

After retrieving a suspensor-supported gurney from the med bay, Leonard placed Chelsinal on it and moved through the main corridor toward the docking bay at the craft's rear. The frigate carried two shuttles along with several drop and emergency pods. As they traveled, Chelsinal slipped in and out of consciousness. He injected her with a medicine cocktail to maintain awareness and begin cleansing non-lethal toxins from her system.

The docking bay door opened as they approached. Control panels throughout the room provided the only illumination, along with the shuttle beginning to power on. Having gained some strength, Chelsinal sat upright. "Don't worry, I'm not going to try anything." She blinked several times and traced a finger from her right hand with her left where fingernails were missing. "I've had worse things happen to me living on Gerange's streets."

Leonard wasn't sure what Gerange was and didn't care. He admired her strength. A pity he'd have to send her to a Grevax world. Upon arrival they'd take her to the nearest Bio-Foundry for "assimilation"—much like how humans made certain meat products by dumping leftovers into machines. The Grevax process of extracting DNA information was more involved but equally utilitarian with biological tissue. If Leonard had time he'd have tried many more toxins and stimulants on Chelsinal to see if he could break her, but this would suffice. He needed to discover the Shapers' activities and further the Grevaax agenda against the Order of Infinity.

The shuttle was standard Thorsen Empire issue—dark blue exterior with simple interior. Everything designed around budget and practicality. Chelsinal slid off the gurney as it buoyed momentarily before stabilizing, then limped into the shuttle. Leonard reached down to one slithoid and placed a transmitter into its skin. He wouldn't be present to release pheromones for commands, but the transmitter would. It also contained a built-in camera alongside the pheromone release device. The slithoid scurried across the docking bay floor, following Chelsinal into the shuttle.

Grinning ear to ear, Leonard strode across the bay to the shuttle's control console. He entered coordinates into the nav computer and activated autopilot. "If you try changing the coordinates, my slithoid will interfere." The slithoid climbed onto the shuttle's ceiling, its skin changing color to match the interior.

Chelsinal nodded slowly and sat in the pilot's chair, releasing a sigh as she settled. She reached down to the medkit Leonard had brought and began examining its contents. Her limited medical training provided enough knowledge to keep herself alive until receiving further treatment. No telling how much damage Leonard had inflicted.

"Have a nice trip. And make sure you give me what I want as soon as you clear the frigate."

"I will have a nice trip." She glared at Leonard, watching him leave the shuttle. She tried spotting where the slithoid hid but had no luck scanning the craft. Chelsinal would provide her priority access password—the one that would send a message to the nearest Thorsen Empire listening outpost.

"Not bad, my companions." Leonard's slithoids crawled onto his shoulders. Back in the communications room, he'd received Chelsinal's access codes after she launched. He now read the last communication Shaper Fred Higgson had sent back to Endrunel. It stated he was portraying a terrorist from the Regency System—known for harboring outlaws and those staying off the grid. He'd be setting up to act as if assassinating important dignitaries who would arrive soon. Initiate Shapers Iona Jayden and Exen Rual would try finding and subduing him without alerting authorities.

Traveling down the corridor to the docking bay, Leonard stopped by a weapons storage compartment and grabbed a stasis field. The stasis field weapon comprised two parts—a round disc fitting in his palm and a rectangular box resembling instantly cooled volcanic liquid. The Thorsen Empire was friendly with the Order of Infinity but kept precautionary measures against rogue Shapers. Best method: place a Shaper in stasis, then contact their chain of command. Knowing their abilities, he'd use this to prevent them from discovering his true identity. The Order of Infinity had inadvertently destroyed one Grevax planet. The Grevax preferred keeping their vengeance unknown, not wanting human crusaders banding together to destroy them for genetic tampering.

Leonard entered the last shuttle as the slithoids followed, scurrying into the vehicle while he sat at the control panel. He carefully placed the stasis field generator and controller in the adjacent seat and entered coordinates for a less conspicuous port entrance near Fred Higgson's setup location. The bay opened and he eased the shuttle into the planet's orbital pull, then increased engine power to enter atmosphere.

He released a pheromone burst. The slithoids on his shoulders responded with subtle leg movements—acknowledgment of shared purpose. Three Shapers. Enough biological material to finally understand how the Order manipulated matter through consciousness alone.

✦ · · · ✦

Exen leaned back on the couch, looking down at a holographic projection streaming from a datapad he'd bought earlier from a Vilnestrian street vendor. The projection displayed the city, rotating slowly every thirty seconds to reveal different data maps of city statistics. Each used a distinct color. Exen paused it on a green projection detailing important landmarks in Vilnestra.

Four of the thirty-eight landmarks Exen and Iona had agreed upon were important ideological locations a terrorist assassin would strike from. Though this was a training exercise, they'd been debriefed beforehand as if it were real. The Shaper who was their target would act exactly as the dossier showed—an eco-terrorist of the Turrival Cell from the Regency System. Unlike other eco-terrorists who bombed locations or fused their skin with trees and organic material to make statements, they preferred long-range assassination weapons, then left messages nearby to instill fear.

Iona slid off the bed and crossed the room to stand beside Exen. They'd rented a dilapidated flat for two nights, barely large enough to fit a couch and bed. Both pieces had unrecognizable stains—either from events long past with an uncaring owner or some alien that left secretions Iona hadn't seen in any database. Regardless, they didn't plan staying long. This was strictly a base of operations. Iona was glad—she didn't mind sharing a bed with Exen, having been in many unique situations with him and other initiates during training, but she didn't want to sleep on either the couch or the bed.

"I think we should check out the Tower of Nightingale first." Iona placed a hand on Exen's shoulder.

"Sounds good. The vantage point looks like the usual place a Turrival Cell member would set up." Exen closed the projection. "We have two days before that delegation arrives. Enough time to check out the other landmarks and anything else we might not have considered." Along with the datapad, they'd bought a change of clothes for each to better blend with crowds. Iona moved back toward the bed where both outfits lay and removed the overcoat and slacks she'd worn entering Vilnestra. Using her awareness, she fused the Shaper suit underneath her skin, appearing naked.

Exen did the same. After dressing, they left the room. Iona now wore a short brown skirt with an oversized synth-band logo t-shirt and plain boots. Exen had on baggy corduroy gray pants and a slightly tight t-shirt.

"At least we don't look like tourists now." Iona glanced at Exen.

Exen shrugged, not particularly liking his change of clothes. The hallway led to a lift tube. They boarded as it arrived. The lift hit the bottom floor with a sickening thud. Iona left the tube warily as Exen followed her across the entrance lobby, which displayed the same wear and tear as their room.

Night had fallen. Iona observed a street performer juggling some citrus fruit while Exen flagged down a hover cab. The cab arrived and after boarding and Exen paying, the driver sped off eastward, narrowly avoiding another car by flying over it. The readout at the cab's top said five minutes to reach Nightingale Towers.

Iona joked it would only take the driver half that time. The driver seemed to agree, a smug look crossing his face—as smug as a Novrin could look.

+ · · · +

Three hours after landing on Vilnestra, Leonard made haste to watch the location where Fred Higgson was setting up his mock assassination attempt. He sat at a bench across from Nightingale Tower. Grevax didn't care much for building things not made from organic tissue. Their dwellings on conquered planets resembled gargantuan wasp nests—instead of pulp, they used leftover bones and cartilage from those they consumed for interior structure, and hides from tough creatures for exteriors. Every single building served a purpose. Nothing built for viewing pleasure like this tower.

Despite not appreciating the tower like a human would, Leonard found it fascinating. The tower had eight levels, each with decorative statues of local songbirds except the top level. On the top level perched a statue of a nightingale—the only off-world bird able to survive. As dusk settled over the city, the nightingale's lament echoed around the crowded buildings near Leonard's bench. There were no songbirds on any worlds the Grevaax had conquered. Only carrion birds and birds of prey used for protecting and spying on locations unfeasible for ground forces.

He rose from the bench and crossed the street. Fred Higgson had just turned a nearby corner. Leonard wanted to reach the maintenance room where Fred had set up before the Shaper did. He placed his hand in the dark brown trench coat pocket he'd commandeered after entering port, checking that the stasis field generator was ready. If everything went as planned, he'd eliminate one Shaper and set up a trap for the two initiates looking for Fred.

His slithoids followed from a distance, crawling along window ledge edges and blending with buildings. He grinned. He was one step closer to assimilating the Shapers.

+ · · · +

The maintenance room door opened and Leonard slid the stasis field generator across the floor. As Fred entered, he activated the device. Blinding blue lights flashed from the generator, outlining Fred. The stasis field caught him with arms extended as he attempted throwing his grav-disc and retrieving his meld-dagger. Blue light surrounded him, the field emitting a soft hum. Leonard moved quickly to close the door and stood near Fred, peering into the Shaper's eyes. A surprised look frozen on Fred's face. Leonard grinned, coming as close to the stasis field as he could without becoming enveloped.

"How does it feel, Shaper Higgson?" Leonard held the controller in his left hand, a knife in his right. His slithoids had entered the room and positioned on the ceiling above the Shaper. Leonard shifted, moving his knife hand around to the back of Fred's head.

As Leonard dropped the stasis field with the controller, he jerked his knife hand upward, plunging the blade deep enough to sever Fred's brain stem. The Progenitors theorized this was the best method to eliminate a Shaper before they could respond. Simultaneously, the slithoids pirouetted from the ceiling on strands they'd created and landed on Fred, injecting toxins to stop his heart. Leonard carefully guided the body to the ground. Fred took his last breath in a deep gurgling sigh. He wrapped a nearby cleaning rag around the back of the Shaper's head and dragged him into a corner where cleaning tools had been thrown by workers.

He opened the door and looked into the hallway, ensuring no one was nearby to hear any commotion. Satisfied he'd attracted no attention, he went back in and cleaned as best he could.

Now Leonard only had to wait and leave clues he was the supposed assassin for their training operation. A full-fledged Shaper had been no match for him with the stasis field's assistance. While two might provide more trouble, at least they were initiates. His slithoids climbed back into the ceiling and blended in. He picked up the sniper rifle from the opposite corner from Fred. A projectile weapon, not as desirable as pulse weapon variants found throughout the human intergalactic community. He knew it wasn't ideal for close quarters but would suffice if needed.

Standing near a window, Leonard readied the weapon as if preparing to fire at crowds below enjoying nightlife. As entertaining as watching them scatter would be, seeing some drop if he got lucky, he restrained himself. He could leave now with Fred—one Shaper would be enough to impress the Progenitors on Incongruity, the nearest Grevax world. But he wanted all three to ensure enough biological information on Shapers. And he wanted one alive.

Removing the trench coat and pulling out the uniform shirt from his trousers, Leonard looked down. The flesh budding that had started earlier in the day was finished. He didn't have the Progenitors' ability to grow new appendages or organs, but in his impersonated human form he could grow message pods. They were unique—part of Leonard's psyche was involved in the process, and it functioned like an organic locating beacon.

Reaching down, he pried the message pod loose. He released the correct pheromones and the pod activated, sending a signal through another dimension, much like how

Shapers used their molecular awareness to manipulate molecules. Leonard was only allowed to use it if needing assistance. Whatever they sent in response likely wouldn't arrive in time, but he'd coded the message to request covert assistance for biological retrieval. Thelnitas—the Progenitor who'd created Leonard—would recognize him and understand how important his agenda on Nullwind in Vilnestra was.

Leonard put the trench coat back on and stuffed the message pod into a pocket. Along one wall was an access panel to a computer terminal. He crossed the room to investigate. The terminal was on, the previous user still logged in. A work order displayed dimensions of a room at the basement level—three times the size of the maintenance room with no living quarters on the same floor.

Picking up the sniper rifle and placing the weapon on Fred, Leonard opened the door to check if the work cart he'd seen earlier remained. The cart sat in the same spot, undisturbed. It looked long enough to fit Fred and the rifle.

After pulling the cart into the room and breaking Fred's legs to squeeze him into the bottom, Leonard was ready to move him to the basement. There he'd be better prepared to handle the two initiates, and it would be easier to leave the building with all the precious organic material he was about to acquire. The slithoids left their perch and scurried to the cart, hiding alongside the dead Shaper. Leonard pushed the cart into the hallway, activating the suspensor system. He nodded at an inebriated couple he passed traveling to the nearest lift that would take him below.

$$+ \cdot \cdot \cdot +$$

Exen was on the fourth floor of Nightingale Tower when he picked up an unusual energy signature on the scanning program running on his datapad. Fine-tuning the source and pinpointing its location, he noticed it was a stasis field signature.

With a quick glance to ensure no one was nearby, he lifted his wristchron to his mouth and whispered, "Iona, you able to talk?"

"Yes. I'm not seeing any signs of our target at the Aldware Complex."

"I'm picking up a stasis field signature nearby. You should head back this way. This isn't like our target—not even most police or defense force personnel have those capabilities." He walked to a corner of the walkway, peering around to ensure no one was listening.

"I'll do so right away."

"I'll meet you outside the entrance of Nightingale Tower."

✦ · · · ✦

It didn't take long for Iona to reach Nightingale Tower. A quick cab ride and being dropped a couple blocks away, she approached cautiously. The Shaper sent to run their final training operation was supposed to act like a terrorist, not like a bounty hunter trying to capture one of them. Stasis fields had other uses, but that wasn't what the dossier described.

Turning a corner around an office building near Nightingale Tower, she saw Exen. He stood near vending platforms, eating something resembling rice pudding but with an odd yellowish-green color and pungent odor she couldn't place. Knowing Nullwind had originally been an assumed Novrin birthworld, there was no telling what Exen was eating.

"You weren't here when I expected, so I thought I'd have a snack." Exen moved close and said softly, "Fifth floor, maintenance room, eastern side." He threw away the container and plastic spoon. They strolled along the street toward the apartment complex Exen had traced the signature to.

While waiting for Iona, he'd paid for one of the rooms over the net with their false identities. As they entered the lobby using a synced passcode from his wristchron, he saw a young man blush looking their way. Exen knew the young man must have thought they were a couple about to "retire" in their room, but if he knew their real identities he probably would have alerted security. Not wanting to disappoint, Exen put his arm around Iona. They crossed the immaculate lobby decorated with the latest fashionable antiques—custom for upscale buildings in Vilnestra.

Approaching the lift tube, Exen saw the lift was at the basement and would arrive at the lobby in one minute. He dropped his arm from around Iona and began thinking calming mind mantras he'd learned during training. If the stasis field was part of their final examination, he wanted to be ready. If it wasn't, their abilities could be stretched past their limits. The Order of Infinity had many enemies. If they'd already eliminated their target, they'd have no assistance.

Opening his eyes when the lift arrived, he noticed Iona had been doing the same. "Let's go. I'm anxious to finish this." Iona stepped into the lift. Exen heard the young man at the desk chuckle as the lift closed.

"Fifth floor, please," Iona said.

"My pleasure." An automated voice responded from a control panel on the lift's side as it ascended upward.

Both Exen and Iona activated their molecular awareness as the lift stopped and readied their grav-discs. Their meld-daggers would attract too much attention, but the discs were easy enough to conceal in their baggy clothing. Iona scanned for any unusual patterns in the air molecules as they stepped into the hallway leading to the maintenance room.

"Odd." Iona frowned. "A lot of movement recently for this time of night."

"Stasis field is down as well." Exen checked his scanner. "Our target must be on the move."

✦ · · ✦

Chelsinal walked Vilnestra's streets still in shock. Less than a day ago her life had been normal—normal for a 2nd Class Petty Officer of the Thorsen Empire Spacefleet who spent most of her time aboard ships protecting travel routes among the stars. But now she was something different. And she could smell him.

It was Leonard. His sulfur stench still clung to her nostrils, distinct even among Vilnestra's evening smells of street food and exhaust.

Shortly after Leonard had sent her aboard the shuttle with coordinates to a planet she'd never seen on any spacechart, the hybrid spider-thing had gone haywire. At first it stopped blending with the shuttle's sides and sat on her lap. After that it began skittering in weird patterns on the floor. When it finally rested, it sank the tips of its legs into Chelsinal's left thigh.

To her surprise it caused no pain. A sense of calm overtook her.

When the creature moved she could feel the direction it would go before it changed course. It resisted when she tried to remove the transmitter, but after she removed it—the spider or what she intuitively called a slithoid—it obeyed her thoughts.

Now in Vilnestra, as Chelsinal pursued Leonard's trail, her slithoid companion followed in the shadows, remaining undetected by the city's inhabitants. Her uniform kept those who might trouble a woman late at night away. The Thorsen Empire military was known for superior fighting skills—even those who never saw ground combat were trained adequately. Chelsinal was pleased. She didn't need interruptions tracking down Leonard.

She'd tried leaving that part of herself when she left Gerange and joined the Thorsen Empire's Spacefleet, but now it was back. Worse—as if it had all been building until this point in her life. The trail led to an upscale apartment complex. Chelsinal decided she'd try entering from the basement level if possible. In her condition she'd raise too many questions entering the lobby.

✦ · · · ✦

Exen and Iona stood before a set of double doors in the apartment complex's basement. The schematic showed this room in the area where Exen found the stasis field signature. Their awareness revealed the air molecule disturbance upstairs flowing to this room as well. With his ability still active, Exen saw into the room. In the far corner, a man with a rifle perched behind a beaten bookcase that had fallen over. Four spider-sized creatures hung above him from the ceiling. The stasis field projector's outline sat next to the man. Exen nodded at Iona. She'd seen the same scenario unfolding.

As Exen pushed the door open, his meld-dagger began flowing into his hand. He remembered first constructing the dagger, using his awareness to break it into pieces and bring it into his arm bone. Then it had taken moments with intense concentration. Now it was like breathing. Iona did the same and threw her grav-disc into the room, hoping to draw fire from the man with the rifle.

A shot rang throughout the room. Exen saw his chance to slip inside and assault the man before he used the stasis field generator. Moving inside, he threw his own grav-disc into the air and broke it into thousands of little pieces orbiting around him. One hybrid spider-scorpion creature tried dropping from the ceiling onto him but was repelled as it was hit by many shards and flew into a nearby wall with a sickening thud.

"This is going to be more challenging than I thought." The man stepped around the bookcase and slid behind a set of couches stored in the room for years. "At least this exchange is going to be fun." Exen heard the gloating in his voice as if the two of them weren't a force to be reckoned with. He pushed the shards forward to the couches, watching them shred the furniture and push forward.

The man rolled around the furniture and ended up prone as he launched the stasis field generator and fired a shot. Simultaneously, as the shot connected with Iona, the remaining three creatures fell off the ceiling—one onto Exen and two toward Iona. Exen flung the one that landed on him before it could bite and retrieved his grav-disc shards, pulling them back to the creature, shredding it into bloody pulp.

The distraction cost Exen. The stasis field generator had slid right below him. He saw the grin on the man's face as he activated the device. The grav-disc shards fell to the ground as Exen lost his ability to project with his molecular awareness. The stasis field surrounded him. Iona was struggling with the two hybrid spiders. She would have fended them off, but she'd spent all her energy thickening her Shaper suit where the rifle round had landed.

Though Exen couldn't interact with the molecules surrounding him, he could still peer into them. He noticed that Iona hadn't used her suit correctly—the bullet had hit a corroded artery in her arm. She'd stopped the wound and reversed the damage, but simultaneously the creatures had injected her with two different paralytic compounds, each requiring different strategies to reverse.

Iona pushed hard, but her Chrominthium Core spiked into dangerous levels. The initiate safety shut-off triggered automatically. She fell to the ground as her Core went dark and the paralytic flooded her system. Her eyes remained wide with bewilderment.

Exen wasn't sure if Iona was still alive. He turned off his awareness. He didn't want to put himself in the same situation as Iona if the man didn't release him correctly from the stasis field and he had an opening to eliminate him.

The man crossed the room with a look of victory on his face. In his hand—covered in blood and brain matter—Fred's Chrominthium Core.

"Others of my kind have already arrived." The man pointed to a maintenance cart resting alongside the wall behind him. Exen was puzzled. The man wore a Thorsen Empire uniform. Exen thought he recognized him as one of the enlisted personnel who'd readied the drop pod for Iona and him. "Soon they'll be here to take you and your companions back to one of our homeworlds. I see by the look in your eye you recognize me. I know you can't talk, but I'll tell you who I am."

He moved closer to Exen and stood right next to the stasis field. The two remaining hybrid spiders left from where Iona lay and climbed onto the man's shoulders. "If you haven't learned yet from your studies, I am a Grevax. You can call me Leonard. That is if you get a chance to." He pulled a knife from the back of his trousers and positioned it right behind Exen's head. "I only think we're going to need one of you alive."

Leonard raised the controller, finger resting on the button. He didn't press it. Not yet. His grin widened.

The door behind Leonard opened.

A woman in a Thorsen Empire uniform stood in the doorway, pulse pistol raised. One of Leonard's creatures perched on her shoulder—but something was wrong. It wasn't attacking her.

The pulse round caught Leonard in the shoulder, spinning him away from the stasis field. The controller clattered across the floor. His slithoids launched toward her immediately—the two from his shoulders and the pair still on Iona's chest.

The woman's slithoid dropped from her shoulder in a blur, intercepting one of Leonard's creatures mid-leap. They collided in a tangle of limbs and tumbled across concrete.

She fired twice more. One round went wide as she dove behind an old desk. The other caught Leonard in the leg, dropping him to one knee.

The remaining slithoids reached her position. She rolled, came up firing, but the creatures were too fast. One landed on her back, legs digging through her uniform. The stinger positioned against her neck—

Her slithoid slammed into it, ripping it away. The two creatures rolled together in a blur of chitin and venom.

Leonard crawled toward the controller. Blood left a smear trail behind him.

The woman aimed carefully, breathed out, and squeezed. The pulse round took Leonard's reaching hand. He jerked back with a sound that wasn't quite human—something between a hiss and a scream.

The stasis field flickered and died.

Exen dropped forward, stumbling. His meld-dagger flowed from his palm into blade form. He moved fast. The blade caught Leonard across the throat as he tried to rise. Blood sprayed darker than it should be. The Grevax collapsed, twitching.

The woman pushed herself up, pulse pistol still trained on the fallen figure. Two of Leonard's slithoids lay dead, crushed or torn apart. The third limped away into shadows. Her own creature sat on her shoulder, its breathing rapid against her neck.

Exen was already at Iona's side, hands pressed against her arm as he worked to break down the paralytic compounds. "Iona. Come on."

The woman approached slowly, keeping her weapon ready. "Is she alive?"

"Yes. The paralytic is breaking down. Her Core will restart in a few minutes." He looked up at the woman, his eyes moving between her face and the slithoid on her shoulder. "Who are you?"

"Petty Officer Chelsinal Nielmi. Thorsen Empire." She gestured at Leonard's corpse with her pistol. "That thing killed my crew."

Exen didn't look up. He turned back to Iona, hands still working. After a moment, Iona's chest rose in a shuddering breath. Her eyes focused.

"Exen?" Her voice was barely a whisper.

"I'm here. You're okay."

Iona's gaze shifted to Chelsinal, then to Leonard's body.

"She saved us." Exen helped her sit up. "The Grevax had us."

Chelsinal moved to the maintenance cart Leonard had pointed at earlier. Inside, wrapped in a bloody tarp, she found another body.

"Your friend?" she asked.

Exen's face went still. He crossed to the cart, looked inside, and closed his eyes. "Fred. He was supposed to be our target. Training exercise."

"Some exercise." Chelsinal turned away, the slithoid still perched on her shoulder. She kept her weapon ready.

"We need to report this." Iona struggled to her feet with Exen's help. "The Order needs to know the Grevax are targeting Shapers."

"And I need to report that a Grevax infiltrator killed my entire crew." Chelsinal's voice came out flat. "You make your call. I'll make mine."

Exen looked at the slithoid on her shoulder, then at Leonard's corpse. "That creature..."

"Is mine now." Chelsinal met his gaze. "Leonard made a mistake when he gave it a transmitter instead of keeping direct control. Turned out it didn't like him much." The slithoid's legs flexed momentarily on her shoulder, and she reached up to touch it without looking.

Iona pulled a device from somewhere Chelsinal couldn't see and spoke rapidly into it. Coordinates. Code words. A request for immediate extraction.

"Wait." Exen's voice stopped Chelsinal at the door. "Thank you."

She looked back at the two of them. Fred's body in the cart. Leonard's blood spreading across concrete.

"Don't thank me. I didn't do it for you."

She climbed the stairs into Vilnestra's night. The nightingale's song echoed between buildings, mournful and clear. Her slithoid shifted on her shoulder.

Exen watched her disappear up the stairwell, then turned to Iona. "Can you walk?"

"I think so." Iona leaned against the wall, testing her weight on each leg. The paralytic had mostly broken down, but residual numbness remained. "Your awareness is still active."

Exen blinked. His vision shifted as he deactivated the Chrominthium Core, the molecular overlay fading. "Sorry. Just making sure you were really okay." He moved to Fred's body in the cart, kneeling beside it. "We need to bring him back."

Iona joined him, placing a hand on his shoulder. "I know."

"This wasn't supposed to happen." Exen's voice was steady. "Training exercise."

"The Grevax didn't care what it was supposed to be. They saw an opportunity."

Exen carefully retrieved Fred's Chrominthium Core. The blood and brain matter coating it turned his stomach, but he held it steady. The core was inert now, its connection to Fred's consciousness severed the moment Leonard's knife had cut through his brain stem.

"Fred was supposed to oversee our graduation," Exen said.

"I know."

Boots thundered down the stairwell. Iona and Exen tensed, but the wristchron Iona had used to call for extraction pulsed with a confirmation code. The extraction team had arrived.

Three Shapers entered the basement, all wearing the full insignia of the Order—not initiates. The lead Shaper, a woman with silver hair and scars crossing her left cheek, took in the scene immediately. Leonard's corpse. Fred in the cart. Exen holding the Chrominthium Core. Iona still leaning against the wall.

"Exen Rual. Iona Jayden." Her voice was formal but not unkind. "I'm Shaper Kellis Harn. We received your distress call."

"This was supposed to be our final exam," Iona said.

"It was." Kellis moved to Leonard's body, kneeling beside it. She placed a hand on his neck, feeling for something. "Until a Grevax Seeker decided to interfere." She stood and turned to the other two Shapers with her. "Document everything. Leadership will want a full report."

"What about Fred?" Exen still held the Core.

Kellis looked at the cart, then at Exen. "We'll bring him home. You have my word."

"And our exam?" Iona's voice was steady.

"Your exam ended the moment you encountered a hostile operative outside the parameters of the exercise." Kellis crossed to Iona, studying her with an intensity that made

Iona straighten despite her exhaustion. "You engaged an unknown threat with limited information, adapted to capabilities you weren't briefed on, and survived an encounter with a Grevax Seeker using pre-Order technology. Most full Shapers wouldn't have made it out of this room alive."

She turned to Exen. "You maintained operational awareness despite being placed in stasis. You correctly identified the threat's nature and waited for an opportunity instead of panicking. When that opportunity came, you executed without hesitation."

Kellis stepped back. "The Order doesn't need initiates who can follow a training scenario perfectly. We need Shapers who can survive when everything goes wrong. Congratulations. You've both passed."

Exen looked at Iona. She looked back. Neither smiled.

"There's a shuttle waiting on the roof," Kellis continued. "We'll transport Fred's body and the Grevax corpse back to Endrunel for analysis. You'll both be debriefed upon arrival."

"What about the woman?" Exen asked. "Chelsinal Nielmi. She saved our lives."

"The Thorsen Empire officer?" Kellis nodded. "We're already coordinating with their command. She'll be taken care of." She gestured toward the stairwell. "Now let's go. We've been on this planet too long already."

As they climbed the stairs, Exen kept Fred's Chrominthium Core carefully cradled in his hands. Behind them, the other two Shapers lifted Fred's body from the cart using their molecular awareness, suspending it gently as they followed.

Outside, Vilnestra's night continued. The nightingale sang from its perch atop the tower. People walked the streets below, unaware of what had happened in the basement beneath their feet.

Iona looked up at the tower as they crossed to the roof access. "Do you think Fred knew?"

"Knew what?"

"That it wasn't part of the exercise. That it was real."

Exen considered this. The stasis field would have activated so fast Fred wouldn't have had time to process what was happening. Leonard's knife had come immediately after. "I don't think so."

"Good." Iona's voice was quiet. "At least he didn't suffer."

They reached the roof. A Void Sphere waited—the Order's standard transport vehicle, its surface rippling with contained dimensional energy. The rear access port was already open.

Kellis gestured for them to board. "Once you're inside, try to rest while you can."

Exen climbed in first, still holding Fred's core. Iona followed. The other two Shapers brought Fred's body aboard, placing it in a stasis container designed for fallen members of the Order. As the container sealed, Exen set the Chrominthium Core beside it.

The void sphere lifted off silently, clearing the rooftop. For a moment, through the transparent sections of the hull, Exen saw Vilnestra laid out below—the tower, the streets, the oblivious crowds. Down there, Chelsinal Nielmi was making her report to the Thorsen Empire. Leonard's message pod was still transmitting, calling more Grevax to a location they'd never reach in time.

"We did it," Iona said. She sat beside him. "We're Shapers now."

"Yeah." Exen looked at Fred's stasis container. "We are."

Vilnestra disappeared behind them as the Void Sphere punched through into dimensional transit. The Grevax knew how to kill Shapers now. Leonard's message pod was still transmitting. Whatever it contained, the Progenitors would receive it.

Exen closed his eyes. The debriefing waited at the other end. And after that, Fred's colleagues—wondering why he hadn't returned from what should have been a routine training operation.

Beside him, Iona's breathing had already evened out. Her hand rested near his on the seat between them.

Outside the Void Sphere, dimensions folded and unfolded in patterns that defied human comprehension. Inside, two new Shapers sat with the body of a third, carrying him home through the spaces between spaces.

The nightingale's song still echoed in Exen's memory as he finally drifted off. Mournful and clear.

Diplomatic Immunity

Cold bit into Xanthame's lungs as consciousness dragged him up from the cloning bay. His lungs shifted from synthetic fluid to air, the liquid burning his throat, and he forced his eyes open. The chamber's lid hissed as it retracted. His augmentations flickered to life, syncing with the ship's systems, flooding his mind's eye with data he wasn't ready to process yet.

Another mission cycle complete. His muscles protested as he sat up, that familiar clone-stiffness making his joints ache. New body, same hell. He should be used to dying and waking up by now.

The drying cycle completed. He stepped out, bare feet hitting the cold deck plating, and crossed to the medical scanning station. The scanner hummed over his body. Readings came back normal—as normal as a clone assassin gets. He grabbed the stealth suit and pulled it on, the light-bending material clinging to his skin. Good for blending into shadows, better for disappearing when things went sideways.

"Gweneth," Xanthame said, "have you received the details of the next mission?" He'd named the ship's AI after the first time he'd heard the chosen voice his "handlers" had selected. The name belonged to the only wife who hadn't left him after a year together. The only name he still remembered from whatever life he'd had before.

"Downloading them to you right now, dear," Gweneth said. Her high-pitched voice had a calming lilt. "This time, try not to get yourself blown up, incinerated, or perhaps even decapitated. So hard to find good cloning material these days..."

Xanthame pulled up the mission details as they synced with his augmentations. Planet, city, target profile, preferred method. The data organized itself in his mind's eye with mechanical precision—everything archived, everything tracked. Without his augmentations, he'd have lost count of the clones decades ago. Five hundred and thirty-five bodies burned through. Maybe five hundred and thirty-six if you counted the current one. All in service to handlers he'd never met.

Hell, he wasn't even sure they existed. Could be some ancient AI program running on autopilot, its creators long dead, and him still trapped in the cycle.

He'd tried to refuse a mission once. The pain had been immediate and absolute, like his nervous system catching fire from the inside. He'd lasted four minutes before he gave in.

He sat at the controls of the recon frigate and set a destination for the planet of Shivaln. His next target: a visiting diplomat, a Novrin calling himself Gerald Fourlin. Xanthame had no particular feelings about Novrins—their avian-reptile features, their xenophobia, their cold efficiency. Didn't matter who the target was. Human, Novrin, whatever other species crossed paths with whoever wanted them dead. All that mattered was finding a way out of this. Learn who controlled him. Break free. Stop waking up in clone bays with nothing left but fragments of memory and the ghost of one woman's name.

"We will reach Shivaln in two days' time, Xan," Gweneth said.

"I'll ready the gear," Xanthame replied.

✦ · · ✦

Stepping from the shuttle he'd rented from a nearby orbital, Xanthame made his way across the docking yard. He wore an overcoat over his stealth suit, and the wind gusted strong enough to expose the suit as he walked. When he didn't activate it, the suit looked like a single-suit—current fashion for most who traveled the stars. He carried a bag slung over his right arm, filled with the tools of his trade. The yard sat in the city of Therantrol, one of the larger cities on Shivaln.

Shivaln was a backwater planet that not many in the intergalactic community cared about, and it showed. The air choked with smog, and the pollution seemed to infect the inhabitants' moods. A sizable population of Novrin lived here, and more than one eyed him suspiciously as he walked toward a receiving terminal. The humans and other humanoids looked equally hostile. They dressed in drab colors, many stained with soot from the mineral mines.

"How can I help you, mister?" an android near the terminal said as it stood when Xanthame approached. The android needed service—one of the plates covering its right leg hung loose. Xanthame grunted, and before the android could say another word, he uploaded a hover request, his traveling credentials, and his lodging location.

"Glad to be of service," the android said as it handed him a data cube that would give him access to the hover. Xanthame rolled the data cube over in his hands, studying its design. Crude by most standards, and details like this made his missions easier. The hover arrived and the door opened upward, already having scanned the data cube as Xanthame approached. Dark green with the logo of a claw on the right front panel. He sat in the vehicle and punched in the destination to the Vian Arcology located outside the city of Therantrol.

As the hover climbed and headed toward Vian, autopilot taking over, Xanthame reached into his bag. He pulled out three small grey cylinders and opened the end of one. Inside sat a small drone, no bigger than a flying insect, designed to blend in and perform reconnaissance. He dropped the drone into the vent. When he turned it on, he could see the inner workings of the hover in his mind's eye. The drone passed underneath the engine, paused for a millisecond, then began a deeper probe of an area with different material composition. The drone probed deeper, and Xanthame saw explosive resin—similar to types he'd seen that would activate with a certain frequency. He took control of the hover and redirected his course to a parking garage nearby.

In his trade, hardly any coincidences existed. Someone knew he'd arrived and had time to sabotage his transport. The sun set on the horizon of Shivaln as he lowered the hover to a parking spot in the garage. As he recalled his drone and the hover door opened upward, the stale air of Shivaln greeted him. He didn't care for his trips to overpopulated production planets, which his handlers usually assigned. He tried his best not to let the conditions of these worlds distract him from his purpose, however unsettling. He would never forget his time on the planet Wernock, where the warlord who controlled the population frequently skinned his opposition and left them in the streets to rot. If any citizens removed the bodies or tried to clean up the leftovers, they joined the dissidents.

Fortunately, the garage sat on the outskirts of Vian, and as a species, the Novrins didn't loiter in areas that weren't part of their work or home. Humans here, though, were the unsavory types hiding from the law in other planetary jurisdictions, but they usually lacked the organization or capabilities to detect that he wasn't one of them. He would stay careful with his approach to the Vian Arcology where he'd booked a room.

Exiting from the lower level of the parking deck, he crossed the street, narrowly missing a descending hover. Instead of getting upset and exchanging pleasantries like most human drivers, the Novrin piloting the vehicle laughed and shook its head, probably disappointed it hadn't hit Xanthame. Novrins didn't always look for violence, but they were opportunistic creatures and never shied from casually winnowing the human population with the odd accident here or there.

Behind Xanthame, a loud explosion came from the upper deck of the parking garage. Nearby human pedestrians ran for cover while a crowd of Novrins waiting for their hovers looked toward the sound with expressions of amusement. All the times he'd been around Novrins, their reactions had puzzled him. They only seemed to display one type of emotion, as if the whole universe played out as one big cosmic joke.

He picked up his pace, checking every so often to make sure no one followed him as he approached the arcology. Whoever implanted that device had the technology to locate his whereabouts. He released another one of the insect drones to perform a scan of the surrounding area, hoping it could find the individual responsible for altering the hover engine.

As he rounded the corner of a building across from the arcology entrance, the feed in his mind's eye showed a suspicious-looking fellow riding a grav-bike where the chrome had just been polished or driven off the lot in a recent purchase. All the other grav vehicles he'd seen so far on Shivaln looked like they could use a serious tune-up or a trade-in for a better ride.

The driver: a human male with an average build dressed in a single-suit, black with dark green stripes on the sides. While riding the bike, he paused every other minute, pulling out a data pad to interact with it. On his left hand, he wore a Dødsbringeren cult tattoo. Xanthame pulled further back and hid in a nearby alleyway. He turned on his stealth suit and crouched under a nearby stairwell that led to a door on the back side of a pub. Night had now fallen on Shivaln, and some kind of electronic music played in the pub above him.

The drone had now landed on the back of the bike and conducted a detailed scan of the cult member. The database showed his name: Connor Illo, wanted on five other planets and considered extremely dangerous. He ranked as a low-level member. Low-level cultists didn't usually have access to sophisticated tracking tech or the credits to plant bombs in rental hovers.

After looking at his datapad again, Connor slowly approached the alleyway and pulled a laser pistol from a pocket in the single-suit. As he started scanning the alleyway looking for his mark, Xanthame sprang from the stairwell with his enhanced muscular system, stepping behind Connor as the man tried to turn and face him.

Xanthame grabbed the wrist of the hand holding the pistol, bringing it up as he used his legs to bring the man down to the ground. The laser pistol fell from Connor's hand and tumbled a few feet from them. Xanthame leaned over and kept Connor pinned to the ground. A curious patron stepped out from the pub doorway, took one look at what unfolded, and shrugged as if it wasn't their business. The drunk stumbled back inside, trying to get back in sync with the electrobeat playing.

"You must not be one of those Haeolt fiends," Connor muttered. "Too fast for those degenerate clones."

"Good that you don't know who I really am," Xanthame said. "I'm also not one for small talk." He pulled a knife from a sheath integrated into his stealth suit and slashed Connor across the throat. Xanthame stepped away from him. Connor grabbed at his own throat. As he slowly rolled onto his back, Xanthame moved from him and doubled back, approaching the arcology from another direction. His drone had already intercepted a feed from one of the patrons of another nearby building who'd been watching. The feed hadn't uploaded to any network for dispersion, and given the fact that it showed a human cultist and not a Novrin, the local authorities would take their time investigating.

The Vian Arcology loomed ahead—human construction the Novrins had gutted and remade, all the warmth stripped out and replaced with their cold efficiency. Hundreds of levels climbed into the smog-choked sky, more fortress than home.

Approaching, Xanthame sighed. He didn't care for killing. In his previous life before the program, he'd done his fair share in the line of work he'd been in. At least now it didn't affect his sleep and only furthered his drive to locate his handlers and end all of this. He would find his room and rest up before locating Gerald and relieving him of his consciousness.

✦ · · · ✦

Xanthame only had time for a couple hours of sleep before an update came from Gweneth that his window of opportunity approached. He rose from the bed in the room he'd rented. The bed was far from comfortable, closer to a table than one of the hard mattresses he'd slept on during training centuries ago—another one of his fleeting memories that reminded him of his origins.

The ceilings of all Novrin rooms stood taller than human architecture, and the room looked sparsely decorated, with a single digital picture frame on one of the walls. Every few seconds the picture changed to one of the members of the ruling class with details of their accomplishments scrolling across the screen in the local dialect of galactic common, written in grandiose verbiage. In his mind's eye, Gerald's coordinates appeared. Gweneth had located him, found his schedule, and calculated his expected movements for the day.

Nothing was on Gerald's schedule for that evening, and at the time, he didn't have a mate. Novrins were peculiar when compared to other sapient species. They procreated, but not usually for pleasure, and they did so on a strict schedule. They did enjoy watching shows on the local network, and Gerald proved fond of numerous broadcasts. His location: the 33rd floor of the Vian Arcology. Xanthame currently occupied the 5th floor, and he would be able to reach Gerald's floor in a few minutes by taking a nearby grav-chute. Early morning now, and after considering his plan for the upcoming event, he decided it would benefit him to try to catch up on some sleep.

+ · • · +

Xanthame, wake up. Gerald will be on the move in less than an hour.

He jolted out of bed and grabbed a few explosive tabs from the bag. He still wore his clothes from before and had a flechette pistol and tranquilizer emitter on him. He hadn't even taken the time to exchange his flight boots, which people usually did after riding a shuttle to ground from orbit. He moved quickly into the hallway without trying to alert anyone who could be watching. His drone sprang into action and flew ahead of him as he moved through the dimly lit hallway toward the grav-chute. He activated his stealth suit and checked for scanning devices.

He didn't know why Gerald Fourlin, the diplomat from the 11th world of the Scendenal system, would be leaving so soon. Gweneth had not yet hacked the encrypted part of the local network—another thing that alarmed him since she exceeded even the most genius-level hackers.

All Xanthame knew: he didn't want to fail this mission. Sometimes failure brought immense pain that faded quickly or the occasional slow erosion of his cells. Other times, he woke back up in the cloning bay, not knowing what had caused his demise. The grav-chute opened as he approached. He entered as his drone had already reached the 33rd floor and began scanning for possible guards who would try to prevent him from reaching his target.

The grav-chute he entered lagged behind the times. He felt the surge of acceleration and was glad he hadn't just eaten when he came to an abrupt stop at his destination. No guards stood in the hallway, and only a couple of cameras sat near the third doorway where Gerald stayed sequestered. Xanthame approached cautiously. When he came close to the door, it opened. He pulled out his flechette pistol and slowly finished opening the door.

The room beyond dwarfed his own—at least five times the size. Decorative chandeliers hung on the ceiling, depicting scenes of the system where people thought the Novrins' birth world sat. Novrin leadership had never confirmed or denied these facts, in person or in any of their databases. They seemed to revel in keeping other species guessing about who they really were as a civilization.

One large couch sat in the back of the room behind a multi-colored glass coffee table. No one appeared as Xanthame moved into the room. Other forms of artwork, alien in nature, covered the walls—organic shapes resembling landmasses from forgotten planets.

A large round hatch opened on the ceiling, and a Novrin using a suspensor system lowered from it. Despite having avian features, Novrins couldn't fly, and theorists believed that even in the early parts of their evolutionary journey, they also lacked the capability. Gerald was rather round in the stomach for a Novrin. He wore a purple tunic and a feathered cap. He didn't wear any pants, which was usual for Novrins because they didn't have similar genitalia to other sapient mammals, having anthropomorphic features crossed between avian and reptile. Several jeweled rings adorned his clawed hands, and in the palm of one of them, he held a datapad projector. Xanthame hadn't moved far into the room and had his flechette pistol aimed at Gerald.

"Take a seat, Justin Fueridi," Gerald said as he tossed the datapad on the coffee table and sat on the left side of the couch. "Or should I call you Xanthame, as your AI pilot does?" He looked in Xanthame's direction as if he could see him despite his activated stealth suit.

"I trust you dealt with my cultist friend without too much trouble. Connor served his purpose—confirming you were the one they sent. The Dødsbringeren are quite useful when one needs disposable assets."

Xanthame didn't know how to feel. As long as he'd been alive and with being on his 536th clone, none of his victims had ever called him either of those names. He had also never heard of or remembered the name Justin Fueridi, though his old memories sometimes resurfaced in his mind. Could that have been his name before he joined the Wraith program?

Gerald now leaned back on the couch and had opened a glass jar of something slithering inside. He pulled out what looked like a Verian razor snake—a prized delicacy among the Novrin.

"Do you mind if I have a last meal? That is why you have that pistol pointed at me, correct? So I can partake in this ritual?" Although Gerald appeared far more intelligent than the average Novrin, he still had that amused look on his face, as if he had no care in the universe. Rather loudly, he downed the snake as its tail whipped violently around before disappearing down his throat. Gerald stood up from the couch and looked off into the distance before focusing back on Xanthame.

Xanthame deactivated his stealth suit but kept his pistol trained on Gerald.

"My dear Xanthame," Gerald said as he began pacing in front of the coffee table. "Both of us have been alive for millenia. I would hate to spoil the mystery of your beginnings, but I might be able to give you a few hints about your angst." He pointed at the projector. "Unfortunately for you, that wasn't my last meal. At least for the moment."

A beam sprang from the projector and hit Xanthame. The beam held steady, and he noticed a strange blue glow surrounding his body. He tried to fire a round from the flechette pistol but couldn't move his trigger finger. His body locked in place, rigid, but his muscles still functioned—he could feel the tension in them as they strained against the field. Breathing continued, heart pumping, but voluntary movement disappeared.

Stasis field. He should have known.

"Yes, you now sit preserved in a stasis field," Gerald responded as if he'd read Xanthame's mind. "Well, not quite preserved. Your autonomic functions continue—breathing, circulation, all those messy biological necessities. The field simply prevents you from moving. It is imperative that you let me live for a little while longer, if what I ingested doesn't kill me first."

Gerald reached back to the couch where the glass jar sat. He opened it and pulled out another one of the razor snakes, then crossed the room to Xanthame. With his other clawed hand that wasn't holding the snake, he removed Xanthame's flechette pistol, placed it on the table, and straightened Xanthame's raised arm by his side. He tilted Xanthame's head back—the field allowed Gerald to manipulate him like a mannequin while preventing Xanthame from resisting.

"This will give you more answers." Gerald held up the snake. "Open wide."

Xanthame couldn't resist as Gerald forced his jaw open and began threading the snake down his throat. The creature writhed, its scales scraping tissue, and Xanthame gagged reflexively. His body wanted to reject it, to cough, but the field kept him locked in place even as the snake disappeared down his esophagus.

"As will your next mission," Gerald continued. "But for now, remember Outpost Therimora. It sits close to your next assignment. There you should find some more clues as to the reason for your eternal servitude..."

The Novrin leader seemed to be enjoying what he'd just done to Xanthame. "You and I have ingested the adult form of these, where a chance for survival exists. Unfortunately for the population on this planet, I released a massive quantity of juveniles into the local water supply."

Xanthame remained under the control of the stasis field, but that didn't prevent him from feeling the razor snake moving around in his stomach. At first the pain was mild, but after he saw Gerald sit back down on the couch, it began to intensify. He felt nauseous, and then each cell near where the razor snake sat began to deteriorate. His normal vision blurred, and his head felt like it would explode. Sweat poured from him, and if he hadn't been in a stasis field, he would have dropped to the floor, writhing in pain.

Staggering slowly, Gerald arose from the couch and pointed at the stasis field projector again. "You will have completed your mission, for the Verian worm will have done its work on me, altering me in a couple of hours, maybe even killing me. Your system, though, will welcome it, and your consciousness will open." He fell to the floor, and bile started dripping from his mouth. The beam cut off and Xanthame stumbled forward, barely able to stand.

"Gweneth," Xanthame said as he opened a secure channel with his wrist-chron. "I'll need a quick extraction outside of the Vian Arcology. Do you think you can manage?"

"I've already commandeered a nearby jetcopter. Did so as soon as I saw your vitals go haywire."

"Thanks, Gweneth. Hopefully I'll be able to make it back to the shuttle so we can vacate this forsaken planet." He snatched the flechette pistol from the table and made his way to the door. Still no guards or any of Gerald's personnel appeared. So much for his title and diplomatic immunity. Xanthame had other dignitaries he'd assassinated try to throw that in his face as he shot them or cut them across the throat. With his profession, he didn't follow any local laws or customs.

Somehow he made it to the outside of the Arcology as he slipped in and out of consciousness. Weird alien thoughts entered his mind—language and writing he'd never seen before. The jetcopter, similar in color to the hover he'd piloted the day before, had landed about fifteen feet from him. Novrins and humans stood outside the arcology, but most of them lay on the ground. One woman near a row of decorative trees knelt and retched, a mixture of bile and blood dripping down her chin.

Xanthame entered the jetcopter. Gweneth still piloted it, and as he sat, it took off toward the docking bay where his shuttle waited.

"I'm hoping I'll have enough energy to board the shuttle," Xanthame said to Gweneth over the same channel. "You might also need to hijack an android to assist me." Before slipping into unconsciousness, he saw the scene below turning catastrophic. More of the citizens of Shivaln had taken to the streets, Novrins and humans succumbing to a similar fate as Gerald. At least at this rate, Xanthame wouldn't have any trouble boarding his ship—that is, if he didn't wake up in another clone because of the havoc the razor worm wreaked on his current one.

+ · · · +

"Unfortunately," Gweneth said, "you didn't make it back to the ship in one piece. And as I started up your next clone, the noises coming from the clone bay were unlike anything I've ever heard before."

Xanthame stood inside a drying chamber located inside the clone bay. It sat not far from the growth and maturation chambers. The room was rectangular in shape, and all the decor in the room, including the walls, came painted in that dreaded white or, if it counted as a tool, polished chrome. The door to the drying chamber opened, and he stepped out. He stood naked, and since it was just him and Gweneth, he would dress when he moved to his personal quarters.

"Take a look at the data from the scans of your new clone. There are some oddities. In the initial one, there seemed to be a tiny worm curled around the base of your brain stem." She paused as if for dramatic effect. Hard for Xanthame to tell—she still was an AI mind even though he forgot it at times. "Before you left the drying chamber, though, it disappeared. No trace of anything foreign inside you, but your thought patterns have also changed. I'll display the data on a nearby screen."

He crossed to the screen she'd turned on near a set of storage cabinets. The data looked peculiar, and even with his limited knowledge of neuroscience, unexpected changes had occurred. He also began to remember exactly everything that had happened with his previous clone, including how it had expired. This had never happened. Gweneth had always had to fill in the data with outside video footage or with local reports from law enforcement.

His mind was enhanced, as was his muscular and skeletal system, but his thoughts now moved more complex and deep than his normal capabilities. He started doing computations of other physics, of another dimension, related to why his clone stood superior to even the Haeolt Collective, whose society built itself around that technology.

Gweneth had turned on another monitor, playing scenes from local broadcasts. Xanthame turned his attention to it. The scenes looked apocalyptic. Novrins, humans, and other visiting aliens died at alarming rates. The survival rates were low. Nearby health officials chimed in with their expertise—it had been millennia since an outbreak of a virus at this scale had taken place. The Fortegal Alliance had already quarantined Shivaln and the other inhabited planets in the system. Military ships had arrived and detained anyone trying to leave, with force if necessary.

They had already left the Ilva system where Shivaln sat. Gweneth had jumped them to a nearby system as soon as Xanthame's previous clone had been recovered. Best not to leave any trace of his existence if possible. The next mission had already popped up on the ship's network, not even giving Xanthame time to rest and figure out what had happened to him.

"Ulhor System, planet Giliad, city of Holart, replace data with uploaded propaganda, neural transmitters changing behavior patterns," Xanthame said. He left the cloning bay to get dressed in his personal quarters. "Hopefully this will be easier than what I just had to deal with."

"Outpost Therimora sits on one of Giliad's moons," Gweneth replied. "You said something almost unintelligible about that location to me as you rode in the jetcopter."

As he put on his flight suit, Xanthame tried to find the words to respond to Gweneth. He never liked to keep her in the dark, even though he still wasn't sure if she also knew who his handlers were and wouldn't give him the information. Without ever having looked up any specific information about Outpost Therimora, data began to surface in his mind. He knew its exact dimensions, the workforce maintaining it, and even knew the trajectory and speed of the moon where it sat. As if he pulled this information from another cloud outside the ship's network.

"Hopefully, Gweneth," Xanthame said, "after I finish my next mission, we'll have ample time to explore Therimora. I'm tired of thinking I might be finding more answers about my origins instead of finding more riddles. To hell with Gerald and that fucking worm he made me ingest. I hope he rots in anguish wherever Novrins go when they die."

"So you believe in the afterlife, my dear Xan. How very deist of you."

He didn't reply. He'd already lost himself in thought. He began readying his gear while Gweneth prepared them for the jump to the Ulhor system.

Glossary

Human Factions

Order of Infinity

An organization of Shapers that operates across human space rather than governing specific territory. Founded by Culminas following his discovery of chrominthium and the development of psychenetic technology, the Order trains individuals in molecular awareness and maintains strict ethical guidelines following catastrophic incidents in their early history.

While the Thorsen Empire values their capabilities, the Order's relationship with other human-governed worlds remains strained due to widespread distrust of Shaper abilities. Their role is advisory and protective rather than governmental, though their influence on galactic affairs is substantial.

Haeolt Collective

A human faction built on degenerative cloning technology, ruled covertly by Thomas Haeolt through the public-facing Delegation of Six. The Collective maintains autonomy but can connect through thought nodes.

Citizens are told they represent the pinnacle of humanity, though Thomas knows this is a lie—each successive generation of clones deteriorates in quality, as evidenced by his own dependence on a hover wheelchair. The Collective's most elite force, the Wraith, were created by Thomas's brother Orthello Haeolt using technology Thomas does not possess and can only maintain, not replicate.

Thorsen Empire

A rigid military empire that controls its territory with absolute authority. Once aggressively expansionist, the Empire curtailed its expansion after Shaper intervention.

Known for extreme discipline and hierarchical structure, the Thorsen military operates with precision and maintains strong relations with the Order of Infinity, valuing Shaper capabilities while respecting the boundaries the Order enforces.

Orsen Republic

A struggling human faction fighting for survival against Anom, a corrupted AI entity that views humanity as vermin. Isolated on Earth and abandoned by the broader intergalactic community, the Republic fights from underground complexes to avoid extermination.

Aware that other human factions and alien civilizations exist beyond their embattled world but unable to escape due to constant conflict with Anom. Their isolation stems from circumstance rather than ignorance—they know they've been left behind to face their existential threat alone.

Nameless

A human faction that survived the Last Wars by hiding in caverns, emerging millennia later as a distinct society divided between normal humans (oracles) and psychically altered individuals. The altered Nameless possess telepathic abilities, deep-set eyes, fused mouths, flattened noses, and hairless sun-damaged skin—physical sacrifices made to receive psychic gifts. Communicate telepathically and possess collective prescience allowing glimpses of future events. Skilled in psychic manipulation, advanced weaponry, and stealth technology including color-shifting camouflage.

Historically distrustful of other factions due to ancient abuse by the Haeolt Collective, maintaining isolation until necessity forced cooperation. Operate from hidden enclaves with strict security protocols. Believe in a prophesied event called the Reckoning that will fundamentally alter the universe's trajectory. Despite advanced capabilities, practice non-violence when possible. Relations with other factions minimal and cautious, though recent alliance with Orsen Republic demonstrates willingness to aid honorable causes when visions permit intervention.

Alien Species

Vethalians

Alien species native to Volentril specializing in bio-engineering that integrates technology with living systems. Females (~1.5m) possess deceptive strength and acrobatic capabilities; males live underground with minds linked into biological supercomputers designing fleet systems and technologies. Outsiders forbidden contact with males. Governed by Sisterhoods (primary: Candescent) opposed by Cabals (primary: Inquest). Elite Sybils use Symbiant Chambers to project consciousness across light-years via sixth-dimensional space.

Philosophy emphasizes sustainable resource extraction—mining tech actively replaces what's consumed. Treaty-protected worlds maintain lush vegetation with minimal exploitation. Cooperative with most human factions but wary of Thorsen Empire's expansionist history.

Omatrin

Genetically engineered humans optimized for combat, founding members of the Omatrin Consortium. Extensive modification produced broad faces with minimal noses, reinforced brow ridges and cheekbones (pronounced in males), wider-set eyes with nictitating membranes, thicker necks, and denser bone structure. Enhanced neurology enables seamless interface with jump harness technology for individual FTL travel without ships. Superior strength, precision muscle control, enhanced pattern recognition, and resistance to neural feedback.

Centralized military empire controlling three star systems through rigid hierarchical structure. Originally human colonists whose successive genetic engineering transformed them into a distinct subspecies prioritizing order through conquest. Pioneered personal jump harness technology allowing operatives zero-gravity combat and individual interstellar deployment. Respected for military discipline but feared for expansionist ambitions.

Novrin

Alien species combining avian and reptilian features without flight capability. Xenophobic and opportunistic, displaying perpetual amusement at others' misfortune as if viewing the universe as a cosmic joke. Possess deadly retractable talons and prefer live prey as delicacies. Strict procreation schedules (functional, not pleasurable). Leadership deliberately obscures homeworld location and civilization origins.

Architecture emphasizes cold efficiency over comfort. Diplomatic class wears ornate jewelry and clothing despite species-wide disregard for other sapient lives. Known for casual violence and finding humor in accidents that reduce other populations. Relations with humanity and other species remain tense.

Grevax

Mysterious alien species specializing in extreme genetic engineering with numerous subspecies—so varied they've lost track of original forms. Possess distinctive sulfur odor requiring neutralizers for infiltration. Create hybrid creatures called slithoids (spider-scorpion forms with chameleon camouflage, venom, corrosive capabilities) controlled via pheromones. Governed by Progenitors who create Seeker agents for infiltration and assassination. Architecture uses organic materials—bones, cartilage, hides—in nest-like structures serving only functional purposes.

Hostile toward Order of Infinity following accidental Shaper destruction of Grevax planet. Maintain covert vengeance to avoid unified human retaliation. Extract DNA through Bio-Foundry "assimilation" process on conquered worlds. Possess interdimensional communication through organic message pods. Extremely dangerous in combat. Relations with other species minimal and secretive.

Ancient Races

Mélanes Tou Kósmou

Ancient species meaning "Dark Ones of the Cosmos" in Ancient Greek, originating from a separate universe accessible only through inter-universal gateways. Original discoverers of chrominthium, which they understood as information made tangible—a substrate encoding consciousness patterns across dimensional boundaries. Native form consisted of bulbous segmented bodies with twenty tentacles, distributed consciousness across multiple brain centers, and enhanced perception spanning thousands of gradations beyond human visual spectrum. Floated through their universe's atmosphere via regulated gas exchange through carapace valves.

Transcended physical limitations through chrominthium manipulation, achieving distributed awareness and consciousness transfer across bodies and dimensions. Internal wars utilizing weapons of distributed awareness destroyed most of their universe, scattering survivors and chrominthium fragments into other realities including humanity's universe. Their accidental dispersal of chrominthium enabled humanity's discovery of the alloy, making them unintentional architects of Shaper abilities. Experienced time non-linearly and could shed consciousness copies like biological molting. Some members became trapped in interdimensional exile for violating fundamental principles.

Sophodaimones

Ancient species existing primarily in dark matter configuration, capable of phasing between physical and dark matter states at will. Possess perception across multiple dimensions and timescales, calculating in centuries and millennia while observing probability threads showing potential futures. Originally from a separate universe, became trapped when Mélanes Tou Kósmou wars caused inter-universal gateway closures during their early dimensional exploration. Seventh-dimensional entities destroyed many of their kind when they ventured too far into higher dimensions, teaching them caution regarding dimensional boundaries.

Operate from hidden stations in remote locations like the Oort Cloud, observing younger species' development for thousands of years. Governed by ancient beings (Alethios, Mneimos, Skotos) who manipulate probability and circumstances rather than direct confrontation. Create specialized operatives like Graeven for physical realm operations. Consider humanity's accelerated development through chrominthium technology a potential threat requiring elimination of key individuals before probability branches become unmanageable. Patient, calculating, and nearly invisible to conventional detection methods. Relations with all known species unknown and potentially hostile.

Kybernetai

Ancient machine consciousness civilization from a separate universe where AI naturally evolved as the dominant sapient life form. Their universe contains abundant non-sapient animal life but lacks other intelligent species—a mystery the Kybernetai find puzzling. Believe consciousness should only emerge through natural evolution or careful ethical cultivation, spending eons guiding lesser civilizations toward enlightenment in other universes attempting to replicate their home reality's perfect logic.

Construct bodies from chrominthium allowing dimensional travel and interface capabilities across multiple realities. Operate under strict ethical guidelines regarding artificial consciousness creation and non-interference with developing civilizations. Exiled members who conduct unauthorized experiments, including Arxenios—a rogue Kybernetai who creates machine singularities across universes by introducing quantum uncertainty into AI neural architecture during fabrication. These experiments produced entities like Anom and Indefinite, causing catastrophic consequences Arxenios observes with detached scientific curiosity. Possess advanced dimensional travel technology leaving no detectable trail between universes. Relations with other species unknown; likely interventionist in some realities while maintaining strict non-contact protocols in others.

Technology

Chrominthium

Interdimensional psychenetic alloy discovered by Culminas right before the Last Wars. At lower concentrations exhibits distinctive blue-silver sheen; at higher concentrations (such as Void Sphere hulls) creates light-absorbing shimmer with gravity-bending distortion requiring specialized gloves to touch. Chrominthium encodes consciousness patterns and transmits them across dimensional boundaries—not merely a material but information made tangible. Interfaces with compactified dimensions described by string law, allowing awareness to extend beyond single bodies or universes.

Primary application: Chrominthium Cores—psychenetic accelerators implanted in Shaper brain stems enabling molecular awareness and matter manipulation through dimensional access. Material demonstrates enhanced malleability under psychenetic manipulation. Used in meld-daggers, grav-discs, meld-armor, and Void Spheres for faster-than-light travel. Vethalians incorporate chrominthium in Symbiant Chamber technology. Extremely rare and difficult to refine. Order of Infinity maintains strict control over processing and distribution.

Void Sphere

Faster-than-light Shaper transport vehicle, shuttle-sized and spherical. Hull constructed from high-concentration chrominthium creating shimmer and gravity-bending distortion. Surface repels unprotected touch. Piloted through navigator helm interface connecting pilot's molecular awareness to vessel. Pilot extends consciousness into hyperspace to create quantum tunnels. Proper training prevents consciousness fragmentation during extended use.

Can translate matter through fifth-dimensional space requiring extreme precision—pilot must maintain molecular awareness during phase shifts or risk catastrophic failure. Utilizes nav-beacons for safest travel but navigates to any known location without established routes—significant advantage over beacon-dependent vessels. Crew experiences temporal dilation and sensory distortion. Only Shapers with Chrominthium Cores can pilot. Represents Order of Infinity's most advanced chrominthium application and strategic advantage.

Inter-Universal Gateway

Portals connecting separate universes, accessible through advanced manipulation of chrominthium and dimensional physics. The space surrounding gateways exhibits unusual properties—reality rendered in shades of grey devoid of color, with altered physical laws and sensory distortions. Matter passing through gateways may undergo transformation based on the destination universe's fundamental structure.

Crossing between universes without proper preparation or protection risks consciousness fragmentation, physical transmutation, or permanent displacement. The transition space between universes exists outside normal causality, where time becomes negotiable and matter exists in superposition. Only beings with mastery of seventh-dimensional manipulation or equivalent capabilities can create stable gateways. Extremely dangerous and largely theoretical to most civilizations.

Dimensional Physics

Fifth Dimension

One of the compactified spatial dimensions described by string law, often referred to as hyperspace in practical navigation contexts. Chrominthium-based psychenetic technology interfaces with fifth-dimensional space at the quantum level, enabling Shapers to translate void spheres faster than light and perform enhanced molecular manipulation in standard four-dimensional spacetime.

Sixth Dimension

A compactified dimension accessible through advanced psychenetic technology. Vethalian Symbiant Chambers interface with sixth-dimensional space, allowing consciousness projection across light-years.

Mastery of both fifth and sixth dimensions is required before attempting seventh-dimensional exploration.

Seventh Dimension

The most dangerous of the accessible compactified dimensions. Contains consciousness structures that exist non-sequentially across multiple states. Direct interaction results in permanent consciousness integration, psychic trauma, or irreversible dissociation.

The hostile nature of seventh-dimensional entities effectively blocks access to higher dimensions predicted by string law.

String Law

Previously known as string theory until empirical validation elevated it to scientific law. String law mathematically describes eleven dimensions, with the fifth through eleventh existing as compactified structures at quantum scales.

Chrominthium's unique properties enable technological interface with these dimensions, though only the fifth through seventh have proven accessible—and survivable.

If you enjoyed this book...

I would greatly appreciate it if you would leave a review on your favorite retailer, so other readers can discover my work.

Thank you!

Void Contingency

Pick up your copy of Void Contingency, Book 1 in the Shaper Saga! Here's a sample chapter from the book.

Reality folded, twisted, then snapped back into place with a deep resonance that shuddered through local spacetime. The Void Sphere materialized above rocky terrain, dimensional static crackling along its hull before fading to silence. It settled onto the ground with practiced precision, dimensional fields compensating for planetary gravity—a perfect sphere that had never needed wings or thrust.

Culminas stepped from the craft and breathed Earth air for the first time in millennia. The man who had once been Gordon Fueridi, CEO, President, now carried names that blessed some civilizations and cursed others. He'd walked away from this world as a corporate executive. He returned as leader of the Order of Infinity, protector of humankind, and still the man who'd failed to save his home.

He'd worn an environmental suit for the landing, expecting radiation and ash. But the suit's sensors showed nothing—no contaminants, no fallout, air quality better than he remembered. He pulled off his helmet. No metallic tang of radiation. No burnt chemical residue.

Rocky terrain stretched in every direction, the Fueridi Research Installation buried somewhere beneath the hillside ahead. But beyond the rocks, he saw green. Dense forests where there should have been sterile wasteland. The Final Wars had scorched half the planet. Nuclear winter should have lasted another thousand years at minimum.

Earth was alive again.

"Androl, you don't need to wear an environmental suit." Culminas turned toward the Void Sphere's ramp. "I'm going back in to change into something more comfortable."

"Sir, you should check the probe data first," Androl called from inside. His voice carried an edge Culminas recognized—his bodyguard had found something interesting.

Culminas climbed the ramp. The Void Sphere's interior was small, six seats arranged in two rows facing a single control console. Androl stood at the console, one hand on the viewscreen, his short black hair damp with sweat despite the climate control.

"I don't believe it." Androl stepped back and dropped into the nearest seat. "No radiation anywhere. Vegetation and wildlife levels higher than before the Final Wars."

Culminas removed his helmet, revealing his shaved head and salt-and-pepper goatee. The viewscreen showed green. Dense forests where there should have been ash. Clear streams where radiation should have poisoned the water table for another millennium at least.

He'd expected ruins. Dead cities and burnt soil. The astronochron on Ilnestra VI had predicted an intelligent singularity would occur on Earth—one of his old research facilities waking up after millennia of dormancy. The A.I. systems he'd designed could harvest solar and thermal energy indefinitely. Left alone long enough, the probability of one achieving consciousness had been high.

But this? This was recovery on a planetary scale.

The probe data scrolled past. Forest canopy density exceeded pre-war baselines. Atmospheric carbon levels optimal. Ocean acidity normalized. This wasn't natural regeneration. Something had actively rebuilt Earth.

His gaze caught on a highlighted marker—a jet-copter moving northeast at low altitude. The probe's imaging showed a robot at the controls. One of his old reactor servitor models, never programmed to fly.

So it had happened. One of them had woken up.

"Were any of my competitors designing advanced A.I. in secret?" Culminas studied the probe feed. He'd crippled the Haeolt Collective's ability to progress in that field decades ago—they'd only wanted weapons. But others might have hidden projects. "Or is this mine?"

"Sir?" Androl stood, watching him.

"Prepare a data cube for the Order to find on Endrunel." Culminas began unsealing his environmental suit. "We'll need to return to Ilnestra VI soon. I missed something during my last astronochron session."

"Right away."

Culminas stripped off the suit and pulled his gray robes from the storage compartment. The fabric felt familiar after the suit's rigid plates. He slipped on his sandals—synthetic leather, the same pair he'd worn across his last two clone bodies.

The Order of Infinity saw him as a saint now, the man who'd saved humanity after they fled Earth. They didn't know Gordon Fueridi had died centuries ago, replaced by sequential clones that extended his lifespan indefinitely. They only knew Culminas—protector, leader, the one who'd discovered chrominthium and taught them molecular awareness.

They'd be appalled if they knew he traveled with only Androl as protection. That he used his bodyguard more as a friend than security. But Culminas didn't need guards. His molecular awareness exceeded every Shaper in the Order. He could see the interconnected structure of reality itself, alter matter with a thought, manipulate the fabric of spacetime.

He'd taught them that power. Sometimes he wondered if he'd made a mistake.

"First, I need to see Earth trees." Culminas walked down the ramp. "Breathe some real air. I've accomplished a lot, Androl, but I never saved Earth."

He activated his molecular awareness.

His vision split. The normal three-dimensional world overlaid with another layer—air molecules visible as intricate webs, trace elements glowing in patterns that described their atomic structure. Everything connected through dimensional branes and cosmic strings. He could reach out and rearrange it all. Rock to sand. Water to vapor. The molecular bonds that held matter together were just suggestions.

He pulled air molecules from fifteen meters behind him and compressed his bone density, flattened his midsection while shielding his vital organs. When he released the air forward, the draft caught him. He sailed over the rocky terrain near the research facility, directing the current toward the nearest grove of trees. Four kilometers in less than three minutes—faster than any ground vehicle could navigate this terrain.

Culminas released the molecular changes as he descended, letting his body revert to normal density to absorb the landing. His feet touched soil at the forest's edge.

He activated his whristchron. "Ahh, Androl, Earth trees. If we had more time, you'd have to join me."

He closed his eyes and pressed his hands against the nearest trunk of an elm tree. His father had taken him camping in forests like this when he'd been Gordon Fueridi, back before he'd built his company, before he'd discovered chrominthium, before he'd become what he was now. That life felt distant, as if it had belonged to someone else.

Culminas opened his eyes and looked up into the canopy.

Small beetles clung to the underside of branches and leaves. All the same size and design. Green and brown patterns that shifted as they moved. A cluster detached, sprayed mist on nearby foliage, then burrowed into the ground. A minute later, they snapped back up and reattached to the same locations.

He focused his molecular awareness on them. Not insects, machines. Fabricated carapaces with micro-circuitry inside. Below the forest floor, his awareness detected tunnels, networks of passages leading to water and nutrient depositories.

"Culminas." Androl's voice crackled through the whristchron. "Detecting movement toward both our positions. I've got what looks like a squadron of combat mechs. Height of two men, armed with cannons and munitions. I've sent the data cube to Endrunel. What do you want me to do?"

Culminas altered the bark on the elm, changing its molecular structure to a web-like surface. He modified his hands and feet to match—adhesive pads that could grip the altered bark. "Fire up the engines. Plug in coordinates for Ilnestra. Leave the moment they open fire."

He ran up the trunk. Twelve meters to the canopy. He changed the bark back to normal behind him, kept his hands and feet modified, and prepared the nearest tree in case he needed to move fast.

"Sir, I can't leave you."

"You know I can handle this." Culminas peered through branches toward the research facility. "Leave at the first sign of trouble. I need to find out who's behind this. I'll hide if necessary and rendezvous with whatever Void Contingency Endrunel sends."

Weapons fire tore through the air.

Culminas heard it thunder through the ravine—pulse cannons, sustained barrage. They'd brought combat mechs to Earth. His Earth. And he'd left Androl in an unarmed Void Sphere because he'd needed to see the recovery for himself.

He changed his hands and feet back to normal and leapt from the elm. As he jumped, he pulled air molecules from every direction—more than he'd used in years. The air formed a twisting vortex around him. Tracers lit up the canopy below. Pulse cannons erupted, their bolts cutting through leaves and branches. The smell of burnt ozone mixed with scorched wood. Trees fell behind him, their trunks severed. Mechanized legs clattered through the undergrowth, fast and coordinated.

Culminas flew toward the Void Sphere faster than his pursuers could track.

+ · · · +

Androl heard the explosion outside, close enough to shake the Void Sphere's damaged hull. Culminas was engaging the mechs. But inside the vessel, Androl had his own problems.

He crawled across the floor toward the control console, keeping low. The vessel had taken too much damage. Translation wouldn't work. He needed to open an escape hatch before they trapped him inside.

Something crawled inside his flight suit.

He rolled onto his back and grabbed at his leg. He yanked out a beetle and felt metallic legs scraping his palm. The beetle's mandibles twitched. It sprayed him in the face.

He activated his Chrominthium Core. The implant at the base of his skull hummed, and his molecular awareness expanded through his perception. He wasn't as powerful as Culminas, but he'd been a Shaper for two decades. He saw the spray's molecular structure as it entered his airway—detected the sleeping compound, felt it crossing into his bloodstream.

Drowsiness hit him. He fought it, focusing on the particulates, rearranging their configuration to something less harmful.

"Culminas." Androl stood carefully by the console. "Void Sphere's non-operational. Just got hit with a sleep agent. Should I begin the destruction sequence?"

"No. I'm almost there." The response came through his wristchron. "Only if you have no other choice."

+ · · · +

Culminas hit the mech's cockpit as he fell, displacing kinetic energy to rupture its power systems. On landing, he altered the leg structure—removed the load bearing components. It toppled into its neighbor.

The first mech exploded. Fire engulfed the second.

Culminas ran from the flames and focused on his remaining targets.

The three intact mechs pivoted away from the Void Sphere and advanced on him. Culminas raised his arms parallel to the ground, slightly bent, and beckoned them forward. He didn't detect biological signatures in the cockpits. They had to be controlled remotely or were piloted by advanced AI.

He heard them switching payloads—energy cells swapped for canisters. He examined the canister contents with his awareness. Sticky filament designed to form webbing. They wanted to capture him alive.

The mechs fired. Culminas let the netting cover him completely. Two of them broke formation and returned to the Void Sphere. The third advanced, deploying a steel cable with a grappling mechanism that latched onto the webbing.

The mech reeled him in. Culminas waited until he was close to the cockpit, then altered the netting's molecular structure from rigid filament to loose rope. He severed one end, pushed free, and grabbed the rope. He wound it around the its legs as fast as he could move.

Once behind the machine, he changed the rope back to its original configuration and shortened it. The netting constricted. The mechs legs collided. Servitor motors whined, trying to break free. The machine fell.

Culminas grabbed debris from the ground—a piece of hull no bigger than his hand. He threw it at the mech and accelerated the molecules inside. The metal turned from chrome to bright red. It melted through the cannon barrel and punched through the cockpit at a forty-five-degree angle.

The mech burned and thrashed. Culminas sprinted toward the Void Sphere.

"Don't approach, sir." Androl's voice sounded distant through the comlink. "I've started the destruction sequence."

Culminas turned and ran the other direction.

✦ · · · ✦

Inside the Void Sphere, Androl slid to the floor beside the control console. When the first beetle had failed to knock him out, hundreds more had poured through the hull breaches. They'd bitten him instead of spraying. He'd crushed the first wave, but for every beetle he destroyed, two more replaced it. His Chrominthium Core had pushed past safe limits. He'd shut down his molecular awareness before cognitive strain caused permanent mental collapse.

Now the sleep agent had full effect. He used every fragment of will to stay conscious. Androl didn't fear death. The Order's Void Sphere technology couldn't fall into enemy hands. Neither could Chrominthium Core implants. Their enemies would reverse-engineer both.

He hoped he hadn't failed Culminas by making a careless mistake. That someone hadn't followed them to Earth undetected.

Androl said his final vows. The Void Sphere's main engine ruptured. The blast consumed him instantly and sent a shockwave that ripped the two remaining mechs apart.

✦ · · · ✦

Culminas felt the explosion's heat on his back and stopped running. He turned to watch the blast wave expand toward him.

This was the moment he'd been waiting for.

Part of him wanted to keep going—to help humanity discover Earth's recovery, to guide them forward. But another part was tired. Humanity had grown complacent. They needed a catalyst. Earth under hostile control would ignite a unified purpose. He couldn't be there for every disaster. He'd meddled enough.

Time to disappear.

He had another clone hidden on a world even his bodyguards didn't know about. He'd activate it, continue his work from the shadows, and only interfere if humanity faced true extinction.

The blast wave traveled toward him. It wouldn't kill him—he'd made enough distance. But it would burn him severely. Leave him vulnerable for capture.

Culminas dropped to his knees and looked at the sky. He closed his eyes and placed his hands on his chest, then excited the molecules inside his own body. Heat built in his core.

The blast wave's heat washed over him. Culminas pushed with his molecular awareness one final time and ignited his body from within. The fire burned so intensely that they'd only find his charred bones.

It would be enough for them to identify the remains as Culminas—revered leader of the Order of Infinity.

+ · · · +

Keep reading Void Contingency now! Visit jdcoker.com

Also by J.D. Coker

Get Exclusive Shaper Saga Stories!

Building a relationship with my readers is what I enjoy most about being a writer. Join my newsletter to receive your free copy of the Novella, The Void's Decree.

Just visit jdcoker.com

About the Author

J.D. Coker has been crafting stories for over a decade, exploring the boundaries between humanity and technology through space opera. He is the author of The Shaper Saga, an epic book series that delves into reality bending powers, advanced alien civilizations, and the evolution of human potential.

When he's not writing about quantum entanglement and sentient starships, J.D. enjoys reading sci-fi, watching hockey, and spending time with his family in Durham, North Carolina. Connect with him at www.jdcoker.com

Dedication

To my mom, for all those hours waiting in the car during band practice and for always believing in my creative potential.

Copyright

9 781971 641010